THE GOVERNORS

Sian Hayton was born in Liverpool in 1944, and studied music and drama in Glasgow as well as becoming a Master of Education in 1977. Married with three children, she supported her writing career for many years with teaching (in the field of developmental psycholgy) as well as with catering jobs.

Her first book *Cells of Knowledge* (Polygon, 1989) won the 1990 Saltire Award for the Best First Book by a new author, and was also published in the U.S.A..

Sian Hayton now lives in Kirkcudbright.

THE GOVERNORS

SIAN HAYTON

illustrated by

BARBARA ROBERTSON

BALNAIN BOOKS

Printed and bound in Britain by BPCC Wheatons, Exeter

The publisher gratefully acknowledges subsidy from the
Scottish Arts Council towards the publication of this volume.

Published in 1992 by
Balnain Books
Druim House,
LochLoy Road,
Nairn IV12 5LF

British Library Cataloguing in Publication Data
A catalogue record for this book is available from
the British Library

ISBN 0-872557-14-7

Dedication
This one is for George

1

Man's a Ribald, Man's a Rake; Man is Nature's Sole Mistake.

Hester planned every meal in detail a week in advance. Furthermore she would never repeat a meal within a month. The cupboards were always neatly stacked with tins; there was always cooked food in the deep-freeze in case she got caught out by unexpected guests. She never was. Nobody ever dropped in on Hester and James, her husband. The one or two who had done so had been met with a sincere but woeful welcome from James whose long sallow face and drooping moustache were not designed to register cheerful bonhomie. Hester frankly looked near to panic.

She found social gatherings of any kind very taxing. Certainly she was stimulated by company, but she passed quickly from stimulated to persecuted. Unless she had a couple of drinks, which gave her heartburn, she would lie awake for hours after any gathering. Tossing and turning, she would fret over the events of the evening,. wondering what so-and-so had meant by some remark; if she had done enough to help the hostess; if her dress had been too casual or not casual enough, and so on and on. This insomnia was very silly, she knew, but she couldn't stop it.

Now, faced with the prospect of an evening with the neighbours she went through her long preparation ritual to put herself in the right frame of mind. At seven o'clock, when Robin, her nearly-one-year-old was asleep she put the rollers on to heat, started to run the bath water and undressed slowly. With the rollers wobbling in place she climbed into the bath and made herself relax. The water supported the weight of her gravid belly and when she closed her eyes and lay back she could almost forget that she was pregnant. She raised and lowered her bottom to push the water back and forth in waves and watched it swirl towards her between her flattened breasts. She pressed her arms against her sides to shove her breasts upwards and studied the landscape thus produced.

"Two foothills and a vast, smooth mountain." she thought. "I wonder what it would be like to explore there. Tricky — kind of boggy I should think — and slippery underfoot."

She closed one eye and tried to see a baggage train fighting its way up the pass of her cleavage. She could almost hear the muleteers swearing and lashing the struggling beasts and she speculated what kind of trade-goods they might be carrying — furs perhaps...

James knocked on the door.

"What is it?" she snapped.

"It's half-past seven," came his hoarse whisper, "You'll have to hurry!"

"Alright!"

Wondering why he always had to disturb her just as she was getting comfy she began to slide the soap over her geological features.

Back in the bedroom she sat at the dressing-table and considered her face. It was scrubbed shiny, and to her it

seemed formless and devoid of meaning with its un-
blemished skin and large grey eyes. She found it as
unappetising as something that had been preserved in a
bottle too long. Her task was to trace lines on it and colour
it in. There was a real face there, somewhere, and she
must find it and show it to the world.

The bottles on her dressing table were arranged in rows
by colour and size. The sight of the three stepped columns
of blue, pink and white bottles was like a calming mantra.
They were the sacramental objects by which she controlled the world.

She raised her arms and began to weave the charm.
Tension left her as she stroked moisturiser into the skin
round her eyes and mouth, as smoothing the muscles
there eased the rest of her body. The big jar of cream,
newly opened, invited her to dig her hand right into its
heart and squeeze the cream between her fingers, but she
stifled the impulse as impractical, not to say childish, and
possibly even disgusting. She wiped her hand on a tissue.
With skinny black brushes, tiny pink sponges and pads
of cotton wool she dabbed and stroked red, pink and
eggshell brown. Her fingers dipped into pots and flew
over her eyelids — a streak of violet, a dab of pink, a
smear of grey and a tiny line of white; a dust of pink at
the temple, white at the chin, then carefully, carefully,
holding her breath, she painted her mouth into a great
bruised plum.

She sat back with a smile of recognition at the result
and saw the reflection of James watching her.

"You do that very well," he said.

"I ought to — I get enough practice."

"Every day, three hundred and sixty-five days a year."

"Sometimes twice a day," she said, drily.

"Will you be much longer? Tracy's here."

Tracy was the baby-sitter — young and sleek.

"I'm being as quick as I can," she told him and

snatched the rollers out too soon. Her fine hair drooped down to her shoulders...

I knew she was trying to get me going — fooling around in the bath like that — but I managed to even the score at the party. Ronnie, the neighbourhood fat-man was making the usual demands for attention. She had parked herself on a straightbacked chair and was gazing out at the golden triangle of sea glinting between the houses. And her defenses were down. He came up behind her, put his hands on her ribs, almost in her armpits, and started to lift her. She stiffened in case he might feel dampness on her. He bent forward to whisper in her ear so that everyone could hear and admire his repartee.

"C'mon Hes. You can't hide away here all night. I need you."

He led her over to the soggy chesterfield and she giggled and sank into its clutches. He slithered down beside her. She told me she was behaving like a jerk because it was his party. I told her she was behaving like a jerk because she was a jerk.

"And how's the prettiest woman in Invergare, to-night?" he asked, grinning at her.

"I'm not the prettiest," she replied with more truth than inspiration. She was attractive alright, but would never pass for beautiful. She was built more for comfort than speed, if you know what I mean.

"Okay — how's the prettiest pregnant woman in Invergare?" he persisted. She giggled again obligingly and we watched his face as he talked. At twenty-eight he's too young to have a stack of double chins, but

they're there alright — lurking under the soft white skin of his throat, trembling when he laughs with their own silent laughter, ready to erupt in their own time. But if he lost weight he would need a personality transplant. He and his bulk are part of each other and even though it will kill him he won't give up an ounce.

He always flirted with her at parties. She once asked James if he minded and he shrugged and said it was okay. If other men wanted to flirt with her it proved she was worth having. All the male exhibitionists of the neighbourhood sought her out because it was easy to fluster her and she didn't have any smart answers to put them on the spot.

She noted with relief that Ronnie had started to talk about his children. She knew she wasn't smart enough to see to it that flirting didn't end in a wrestling match. The chances of him getting physical were as likely as rocking-horse shit. I could have told her if she had bothered to ask. What he likes is talking about his kids. He's got five of them. No wonder his wife likes her vodka.

Feeling the pressure off her Hes relaxed. With an invisible writhe of pleasure she lowered her eyes and tuned him out. This way she had of sitting silent had got her the reputation of being a good listener, only she wasn't listening. She was reviewing the week. I left her to it. That kind of thing bores the ass off me...

...Tomorrow was Tuesday — washing day. Hester broke with tradition here because she thought that everyone using water to wash on the same day could not be a good thing.

She had alarming visions of a Monday morning when the level of the reservoir above the town drops three feet, the gulls on the surface descending startled like people in an express lift. After an hour's churning pause a flood of white pours out into the sea when all the washing machines empty at once. She knew this was ridiculous.

"Soap-suds go into the sewers before they get to the sea. They wouldn't appear white in the sea."

She told herself this, but the notion had a grip on her and she pictured the foam in torrents, bursting out beside the pier, bobbing and swishing among the pillars and on out to sea — a procession of creamy slime streaking the waves. At this point she would have to cram her mind shut and concentrate on something soothing like the weekend shopping list.

She never let anyone know about her boisterous imagination since she thought it made her a bit weird. Like her real name, her bloody name, that had been willed on her by a whimsical father dead nearly twenty years. They were both something to be wished away. Her father had been a moderately unsuccessful academic — his sense of the ridiculous stood in the way of promotion — who taught marine biology to bored and boring students. Being unable to transmit his feeling of wonder to those who were obliged to listen to him, he had turned his attention to his elder daughter. In case she at some future time should find herself captivated by marine life he had named her Hesione. Then, before he had time to show her the meaning of this talisman he was killed in a car crash driving home. She could always picture him at that last moment, his eyes fixed on the sea from the first glimpse on the homeward journey —

"Look Hesione — there it is now. Nearly home."

And as he lost consciousness for the last time she felt his grief and rage that he had not made it to the sea shore.

She was snatched back into the present by the sudden silence that had fallen. Ronnie must have asked a question. She rummaged through her mind but couldn't find a trace of what he had said so she gave him one of her best smiles and handed him her glass.

"Ronnie, dear, I'm awfully tired. D'you think you could get a drink for a pregnant lady — one for the road?"

"One for the gutter, eh pal?" he said, and pinched her cheek. "What are you on? Spritzer's — right?"

"Not too strong, please."

He returned with a glass of nearly pure wine. It was time to plead her condition and leave, but Ronnie was convinced his youngest, at a sprightly eighteen months, was showing signs of genius.

"Remember, he walked before he was a year old. Now he's got a huge vocabulary — more than three hundred words I reckon."

As she waited for him to get to the point she wondered how he managed to count them. She could imagine him running after the poor, pestered wean with a notebook and tape-recorder. He came to the punch line.

"Could you do that — could you ask your mother?"

— ahh, that was what she'd missed before, "She would know if he needs special education. With all her years in teaching she must have seen some special abilities."

"Where my mother works it takes her all her time to get through the normal curriculum."

"I don't know how she does it," he said sulkily. "She could easily get a head-ship."

"She's got a strong sense of duty. She feels they need her."

He was about to get disappointed and difficult so she went on.

"I don't know if there is a school that deals with specially bright kids, but I'll ask her. Okay? If there is such a thing she would probably know about it."

"Great!" he made a dive to hug her and she jumped to her feet. He stood and ran his arm round her waist as far as her mountain. She looked round for James and saw him by the window alone looking out into the garden.

"Lucky bastard," she thought — the wine was taking a hold. "Thank God he's not talking to anyone. We can get away."

That night she dreamed she was standing on the bank of a river. The water was so clear that even from a distance she could see the stones on the bottom — grey red and green — some speckled with mica that sparkled, some banded with white quartz. The tiny green weeds that grew amongst them were quivering with life, and the silver fishes that swam among them glittered, iridescent.

She felt sure that if she picked up water in her hand it would clatter as it fell on the stones. She could see why water is classified as a mineral. The gently flowing stream below her was moving crystal. She stood on, and quiet surrounded her.

Downstream a tree dipped to touch the surface. She started to move toward it to see what effect this contact would have on the water when a movement upstream caught her eye and she stopped to watch. It was a human and from the length of her hair a female, swimming downstream with an unhurried breaststroke that hardly disturbed the surface of the water. Hester scrambled up the bank to get a better view of the swimmer and saw with a slight shock that she was naked. Her hair was pale brown and merged with her back so that her neck and shoulders smoothed off into one curve. Since she was face down in the water and her arms and legs never broke the surface Hester could not identify her, but as she came closer she became more and more certain that the woman was herself.

This fact caused her no surprise, though she felt it should, and raised her eyes while she considered it. Now she saw for the first time the stretch of river where the swimmer was heading. Where the branches touched the water it began to lose its clarity, and twigs and leaves floated on it. She moved along the top of the bank with the speed of a dream and saw that past the trees the water was even dirtier. The river narrowed, the banks on either side grew steeper, and she realised the bank opposite was a rubbish tip. There plastic sheet fluttered and nameless rusty metal shapes jutted into the water. The bank was a sheer slide of mud and rubble and rotted grass. The swimmer came steadily on, oblivious.

Hester knew that the other could not see the murkiness of the water she was approaching. If she could have, surely she would have stopped. Frantic, she looked on downriver. There she could see things floating on the surface — blobs of fat brown scum, dirty paper, plastic bottles, and then, almost faint with disgust, she recognised excrement. She tried to shout to the swimmer but her mouth was sealed, and all she could get out was a moan. The swimmer was getting near the rusty metal. Hester ran along the bank to see if she could find someone to help. Something must be done to stop her or she would choke on the filth that she was approaching so calmly and so steadily. Already Hester could feel the greasy taste of shit on the back of her tongue.

At the end of the bank she found that she was alone. Nevertheless she was reassured, for once round the bend the river fanned out over clean shingle and ran into the sea. Overhead the sky was clear and the sea below was dark blue with white crests blown up by a vigorous breeze. In the rocks at her feet the sun glittered on a large rock-pool surrounded by a shaggy growth of weed. Concentric rings of green reached out over the surface shading from almost white at the edge to dark green at the centre. At the very middle of the pool there was a patch of clear water and underneath this she could see a glinting white crust. A large piece of metal stuck out of the water and bent sharply in the middle. It made her think of a handrail.

"If she can get to that pool she'll be safe!" she shouted in triumph. Eagerly she turned back to the river to tell the swimmer where she should go but something held onto her and pulled her about.

The vivid seascape faded and she woke to find James leaning over her, shouting,

"What's the matter, Hes? Are you alright? Hester!"

"Nothing's the matter," she cried, "Why did you have to wake me? Now I'll never know if she made it or not." And she burst into tears of rage.

James was confused.

"Are you okay? Have you got a pain?" he insisted.

She shook her head and struggled to control the disappointment that had taken her over. She felt a childish frustration that she had been taken away before the end of a film and would never be sure that the happy ending had happened the way it was supposed to.

James stroked her head uncertainly.

"I shouldn't have wakened you — but you were shouting —"

"No, no," she gasped. "It's alright — I'm fine. I'll be okay." She began to calm down, although sobs still made her breathing difficult.

"Do you want to tell me about it?" he asked, without enthusiasm.

"Not just now — in the morning. I think I want to forget it as soon as possible."

"It was just a dream, then?"

"Yes, that's all. If I go back to sleep quickly I expect it'll disappear."

As they lay close together in the darkness he said,

"I think maybe the party tonight wasn't such a good idea."

"I can't shut myself up just because I'm pregnant," she

said to reassure him. "Pregnancy is not a disease."

The next morning, to her surprise, she awoke feeling rested and cheerful. The dream had left no emotional residue and the feeling of panic had dispersed.

The morning routine took over.

James showered; Hester cooked; Robbie played in his cot.

Jamed ate; Hester fed Robbie.

James drank coffee; Hester showered; Robbie played with his breakfast.

James prepared to leave; Hester followed him into the hall for her goodbye kiss.

"About last night —" he began. He had to say something but had no idea what.

"Don't worry about it. It wasn't really that bad — just very vivid. And anyway I can hardly remember it now."

"You're sure you don't want to talk about it?" He looked down at her and his heavy black moustache drooped lugubriously.

"Oh, no. Really, there's nothing to talk about. I did too much yesterday, and the party on top of it. I won't let it happen again."

"You're sure?" he cued her an old joke.

"Sure I'm sure." She smiled expectantly and he returned a smile and a shrug.

"As long as you're sure."

They both laughed.

She watched him affectionately as he opened the garage and backed the car out. It was kind of him to worry about a bad dream.

"I must have been making a terrible row," she thought. "I'll have to watch it in future."

She waved energetically at the car as James drove off into the bright morning, then turned her thoughts to the laundry.

"It's a good day for drying."

2
Qui nunc it per iter tenebricosum

The following Sunday the Grieves went up to town to visit James's parents. Armed with the few cutting flowers the garden would yield they strapped the baby into the car and took the main road east. The senior Grieves lived, as they had for the last thirty years, in a housing estate outside Glasgow which had been built between the wars. The estate had fallen into a decline over the last few years, but the Grieves were unwilling to leave and so put up with the increasing number of unkempt gardens, broken windows and open bin-sheds that surrounded them.

Hester was wryly aware that both her mother and James's parents were puzzled by their marriage. Her sister, Charlotte, said she thought it was a wonderful idea and considering that Hester had taken James from her when she brought him home from University one day, this was pretty generous. Her mother would not betray her egalitarian principles and said nothing when Hester defied family tradition and didn't marry a lawyer or a doctor from lawyer or doctor stock. James was what

Charlotte described as 'aspiring working-class' and he accepted the patronising epithet with a shrug. He was on record as saying that the best thing a working-class boy could do for his class was to prove that they were as good as anyone else. He had taken a degree in marine engineering and joined the professionals. To Hester he had looked as if he would benefit from having one of her taste, education and skill bestowed on him. She sailed into church ignoring any veiled warnings.

Nevertheless it was, and always had been, an effort for her to communicate with her in-laws. Whereas Charlotte and her mother always managed to believe there would be a welcome for them at Hester's, despite her unusual life partner, James's parents always behaved like interlopers. They seemed to think that their place was on the periphery of James's life, and his marriage was like his University degree — an achievement they could only approve of in the abstract. His sister, his elder by ten years, had made the much less unsettling choice of a gas-fitter.

Hester had been dismayed when, before the wedding, James had mentioned carelessly that his parents were planning to give them a suite as well as the washing machine. Her idea of a three-piece suite ran into thousands of pound's worth of leather and buttons, and she guessed that the Grieve's taste and income would come no-where near that. It was preposterous. She had decided that she would go round sale-rooms and build up a collection of interesting old furniture that she could lavish her time on. At last she spoke to James.

"What are we going to do about your parent's present?" she said blushing irrepressibly.

"What do you mean 'do about' it?" He was studying her.

"We — your father — he's retired — they can't possibly afford — you know —"

"Aye, they can. Just you let them worry about what

they can afford. Don't forget they've been saving up for this since I was a kid."

"But it's such a big present — !"

"They gave our Sandra bedroom suite and a carpet for her wedding. They couldn't let the son and heir go off with less."

She was silent for a while, gnawing her lip and staring at her shoes.

"What's the problem?" he asked gently.

"Oh, nothing really. It's hard to say."

He laughed at her crimson face and put his arm round her.

"C'mon, be honest. What's on your mind?"

I told her straight. They had hit a critical moment. If she continued to hedge and drivel on about politeness and money — and there were twenty-odd years of conditioning to make her — she was going to be stuck with something big and ugly and hard to live with and wasn't a three-piece suite. Could she be honest? I told her I doubted it.

"What do you want?" I asked. "For Chrissake say it. If you're going to shack up with him you owe him a little piece of the truth."

"Well," she said, watching his face for any giveaway. "I wasn't really wanting a suite at all."

"You'd get to choose it," he said. He was really enjoying himself. "They would expect that. You can go into town with them one day."

"No! It's just that a suite is so tying. Once it's there you have to arrange everything round it."

In her mind'e eye she could see an elegant assortment of pieces being grouped and re-grouped easily like guests at a smart reception.

He knew what she meant.

"Same as Francoise."

For a moment she stared at him with her jaw hanging in the breeze.

"Don't screw around now!" I warned her.

Finally she grinned. The guy was no dope — we had to give him that.

"Something like that, only not so spindly."

"I'll speak to dad."

In the end they managed to trade for a washing machine and a tumble-dryer. Hester was very pleased and able to show it. More than that, they had managed their first conspiracy, which was fine.

Today the bonds were getting frayed.

Before they left James took Robbie into the garden to pick the flowers and the baby had got muddy.

When he realised he was going to be taken from the garden Robbie, usually a co-operative child, had clenched his fists to stop Hester cleaning them.

Then he screeched and strained at the seat straps and his parents felt hurt. This trip was largely for his benefit as his Granny would make a marvellous fuss of him.

The day was hot and overcast and Hester felt sweat stinging her upper lip as she struggled with the child. She saw trouble ahead and it arrived promptly when James said,

"By the way, are you going to be wearing that old

brown thing?"

"Yes," she answered truculently, "I know it's not the smartest thing I've got, but it's all cotton. I'll be comfortable."

"Ah well, as long as you're comfortable, I suppose —"

"What's wrong with it?"

"It's just a bit — shapeless, that's all."

Indignant she addressed the sky.

"And to think when he married me he thought Christian Dior was a film director." She sighed heavily. "It's me that's shapeless just now. Not the clothes. Nothing is going to look good on me for another four months."

He tried to laugh at that, but she could see he was piqued at being reminded of his early gaffes. Fortunately Robbie fell asleep soon after they set off and they couldn't talk any more. Hester had slept badly and soon started to doze but today she had forgotten to put a cushion in the car and the vibration of the engine drilled into her head wherever she tried to rest it. Very soon nausea was slapping her in the chest and she thought bitterly that at five months pregnant she could be spared this hauling about.

James had decided to cheer himself by taking a complicated route to his parent's house. This took them through the estate and into areas they usually avoided, and as they cut deeper into this territory Hes hunched down in her seat and kept her eyes on the road. The tenements were tall and close together, shutting out light from the bare-earth gardens. The fences were peeling and broken. She forced herself to look up at the buildings. They were brownish-yellow and stained with soot, their balconies hung with washing festooned on bits of string, and the curtains looked as if they were hung the same way.

As they descended towards a T-junction they saw a heap of dirty rags lying in the road. As they approached they saw that the heap was a man in impossibly dirty clothing. James stopped the car and rolled down the window and Hester craned past him to see if there was enough space for the car to get round the body. As far as she could see there was not. She looked enquiringly at James who raised his shoulders in perplexity. He whispered so as not to wake the baby.

"I can't get past. I'll either have to mount the pavement or move the − body. You'll have to go and look. If I get out I'll disturb Robbie."

Grudgingly she got out. On the other side of the main road rusty railings and a straggle of hedge ran round a bald football park. Under the hedge there squatted two children and their faces − grey on grey − confronted her.

"Yiv no' tae move 'im," said one.

"I wasn't going to," she answered, bridling. "What's the matter with him?"

She could see no sign of injury.

"He jist fell an' lay there."

"The brother's away fir an amblance," said the other, who might even have been a girl for all she could tell.

Possibilities about what had happened to the man fluttered through Hester's mind. That he "jist fell an' lay there" seemed least likely. Car accident? Hit and run? These children wouldn't say if it were. Drunk, most likely. She bent over the body. A stunning array of smells hit her nose. First the cat-piss smell of a meths drinker, then the sweet, vile smell of rotting humanity, then, strangely, the flowery smell of unwashed hair and finally, strongest of all came the oily, tongue-coating fetor of decomposing fish. Hester reeled back, gasping. She was sure something should be done for the creature, foul as it might be, but she couldn't think what.

"Hurry up!" James hissed.

"Yiv no' tae touch 'im," the child repeated, indignantly.

"Who would want to?" she snapped. She would have had to steel herself merely to stir the greasy brown heap with her foot, and then only provided she could go home at once and change her shoes.

That still left her with the problem. There was certainly no room on the road to drive past the body, and then again, should they leave? If what the children said was true, then an ambulance was on the way, but she doubted if she could trust them. It was really up to people like James and herself to take charge — but then again what if there were more to the creature's collapse than they said. They would become involved — there would be police asking questions — and what if the children were responsible for the collapse. She would put nothing past them — they were aliens.

She looked back up the hill they had come down and saw two youths hurrying toward them, baggy trousers flapping, skinny arms akimbo. It had to be the brother and friend. Why were they in such a hurry? Surely they wouldn't blame James and herself? One of the youths shouted and waved imperiously.

"Is that your brother?" she asked the children, who stared back, blankly. "Tell him we didn't touch him," she yelled and flung herself into the car.

"You'll have to go over the pavement," she barked as she got in. "Hurry!"

James reversed onto the pavement, threw the car into first and rounded the corner in a spurt of dust. Hester looked back and saw the children doubled up with laughter.

"What was that all about?" He hadn't seen the brother.

"Oh, I don't know — he was dreadfully dirty — I was wondering if we could do more to help."

He glanced at her flushed face.

"Don't worry about it. The kids said help was on its way. More people hanging around would have made things worse."

"Are you sure? Those horrible children —"

"Them? They seemed alright to me. The brother probably left them with strict instructions while he went to the phone. They were doing fine watching the man for him. Very responsible."

"You sound like my mother," grumbled Hester.

"Rubbish!" he exclaimed, loudly. Robbie snuffled and threatened to wake, so he said only, "I went to school with kids like that." And finished the journey in silence.

At his parent's house James did not help Hester out of the car. Her brain was still tramping wearily over the incident 'and she barely noticed that they had arrived. She failed to wave up at the second floor window where her mother-in-law stood, and James woke Robbie and flapped his hand rather roughly at his Granny to make up for it.

All in all Hester made a complete mess of the ritual because when she went in this time she was suddenly aware how cramped the house was. The hall ceiling seemed about to land on her head, the sitting room was unbearably poky and you could stand in the middle of the kitchen and touch all the walls. With horror she struggled to push away graceless comparisons with her mother's house — the drawing-room with its tall windows looking out over mature gardens — the airy kitchen — the elegant tiled hallway. This took up so much of her attention that she hardly smiled at her in-laws, let alone spoke to them and it took a warning pat on the bottom from James to bring her round. Very soon she had been relieved of her jacket, pressed into an armchair, bidden to admire the pictures Sandra had sent from Canada, and handed a cup of tea.

All through the meal, lest she should be caught out again missing cues, she watched her in-laws. She became fascinated by the way Mr. Grieve's gestures seemed to anticipate, or even produce his wife's actions. His knife knocking on a plate led her to hand him the bread; his cup hitting the saucer supplied him with a refill; the crumpling of his paper napkin got his plate removed. There was no doubt who was head of the house.

"How long has this been going on?" wondered Hester. "How long has he been pulling her strings with never a word spoken? Does she know what's happening? Does *he* know? He has no need for words while this slavery continues in secret. Neither of them need know anything about it. My God, do James and I do the same thing? I don't think so. I must take care we don't."

After tea Hester offered to help her mother-in-law but was told she looked tired. Robbie crawled into the kitchen — at least the floor was spanking clean — and she heard his Granny's delighted greeting. He would be given all sorts of inappropriate things to eat — bread and jam — but she couldn't bring herself to go and supervise. She settled deeper into the chair while James and his father swapped gardening notes. It was nearly the only thing they had left in common.

Everyone agreed how tired she looked and her silence was excused. James told them about the trip over and generously said how worried Hester had been about leaving the "old man." They even put on the local radio news for her to see if an accident had been reported. They were kindly people and she told herself she wished she could get on better with them.

Once safely home Hester forgot all the unpleasantness in routine. She settled Robbie in his cot and with a sigh of relief began to read to him. According to her mother, for the best possible start in life a child should be exposed to language from his earliest days. Being by nature garrulous it had been easy for her to administer a nutrient bath of words to her children, but what came naturally to her mother gave Hester serious problems. She solved them without calling on her mental resources by reading to Robbie from her own story books. Chidren's books nowadays, she found, were rather thin on text.

Her books tended to have broken spines from a habit she had in childhood of sleeping with heaps of books around her. Her mother had removed them, of course, but Hester always sneaked them back in. It was like having a crowd of interesting people around her all night, and she kept up the habit until she was married.

Tonight's story was from a really old collection of Scottish legends illustrated with line drawings and colour plates. One of the plates — unsuitable for children — was of a naked woman standing on the seashore. The sea was lapping round one of her feet and her face was turned to the land where children were playing beside a small house. They didn't notice the woman. Hanging from her hand was a piece of something like a cloth coloured in curving bands of red, grey and purple, and the title of the picture was, 'The seal-wife must leave her children.'

The story was of a crofter-fisherman who, one mid-summer evening, happened to see a crowd of people dancing on the seashore. When they saw him they slipped into sealskins they had left lying among the rocks, changed into seals and swam away. The man could not forget them, especially a dark-eyed girl whose gaze had met his for a moment. At last he went to the wise woman of the village to find out how to restore his peace of mind. She told him that the only thing he could do was to capture one of the selkie women by stealing her skin one night when she came ashore to dance. Then he must marry the woman and keep her sealskin hidden. Provided she never saw the skin she would remain a faithful human wife, but the instant she saw it she would return to the sea and never come to land again.

The man did as he was told and for a long time there

was no trouble. Then one day the inevitable happened
— the woman found her skin and went back to the sea
leaving her husband and her children to mourn her. The
man died soon after of a broken heart and the selkie
mother helped the orphans the best way she could from
the sea. The children grew up to be fine fishermen and
pipers.

Hester read the story to Robbie and sat on to finish it
long after he was asleep. In the dim light of the baby's
room he lay breathing softly. His fingers opened and
closed; his eyelids trembled and he sighed. What could
he be dreaming of, she wondered. Probably food as he
had inherited his appetite from herself. He drew a long,
shuddering breath as if he had cried himself to sleep and
her heart was wrung for his grief.

"Is there no time in our lives when we know complete
happiness? I couldn't leave him no matter what might
happen to me. I would stay with my child. That poor
woman — how it must have hurt her to leave the land.
Imagine living between land and sea and never being
content with either."

She sat in the stillness and listened to the noises outside
— the voices of children, the wheeze of a swing, the
thudding of a football. A door opened and a voice called
softly to the children and silence fell.

The child inside her moved suddenly and she had to
stand up.

"Alright. I know you're there too. I won't forget."

She smiled and patted her stomach. For once she was
glad to be carrying a child inside her. Usually the only
comfort she found in pregnancy itself was the fact that
she could avoid sex. Not that James ever knew about her
reluctance. She managed to play the part of an aroused
woman quite efficiently, and he was as inexperienced as
herself when they came to the honeymoon. The only
pleasure she had from his body was that his low-set

nipples made his chest look as mournful as his face. Or that at night when he docked his knees behind hers she could feel his sex, soft as overripe fruit, against her buttocks.

She sighed, stretched to ease the muscles of her back and tip-toed out of the room. At the top of the stairs she stopped in dismay when the doorbell rang and she waited till James opened it. It was Ronnie and Karen. Ronnie saw her at the foot of the stairs, blew her a kiss and waved a bottle at her invitingly. She smiled and wondered what in Holy Hell had brought them round and pressed a finger to her lips to keep him from shouting. James was also baffled for as he showed them into the sitting room he looked up at her, rolled his eyes and shrugged.

Suddenly she remembered and slapped her forehead in rage. The Monday before, slightly the worse for wine, she had made her escape from Ronnie's sweaty hugs by inviting them round — "just the two of them as she wasn't ready for a lot of visitors". Her visions of a serene evening with the television and an early night turned to ashes and was replaced by the certainty of a horrible time avoiding Ronnie's hands and watching Karen getting plastered. In a small group they concluded the evening's entertainment by embarrassing James and herself with detailed revelations about their sex life. James said he thought they were working up to some wife-swapping and shuddered reassuringly. She almost hoped he was right because then she could indulge herself righteously in the gesture she had been saving up for years. She was going to slap Ronnie's face so hard his crowns would fall out.

This thought took her downstairs with a grim smile and she went into the kitchen through the door from the hall so that the company wouldn't see her till she was ready. Tears of rage were stinging her eyes.

3

If you miscarry your business of this life hath so an end.

In spite of her assertions about takings things easy, Hester had planned something special for Robbie's birthday in June. She had used her condition to cajole her mother into giving her a hand with the child managment side and that lady had agreed to give up one of her days off with something like good grace. The party never happened because in the morning of the Thursday before it Hester found she was bleeding. The evidence lay patiently before her in the toilet — mucous with red lines in it. The sight made her recoil as if she had been struck in the face. She went into the bedroom to sit down and to let the thought inch its way into her brain.

"I seem to be bleeding — it's probably nothing — a tiny lesion. Nothing to worry about —

"Oh God, it's really happening to me — the equation every pregnant woman dreads: bleeding= miscarriage= dead baby. And maybe even myself —"

Distracted she got up and went to Robin's room. He

was struggling to get a toy out of his box and getting round to fussing about it. She helped him without noting what she did and went back to the bedroom. Shakily she lowered herself onto the bed.

"Sit still," she told herself, "it may not last."

After a while she went back to the toilet and checked again. There was a red smear like lipstick on her pants.

"Bright red!!" she screamed silently. "Arterial blood!!"

She wished she knew a lot less, or a lot more, about how her body worked. Her heart was hammering so hard that her body shook and the din stopped her thinking. She wanted to hide somewhere, to vanish, to phone her mother and weep into the receiver. To distract herself she spoke aloud.

"No, no. She'll be at school. I mustn't worry her by ringing them. She might even be out with her class. It's that time of year. What should I do? What's the sensible thing to do?"

She began to study her situation like opening up a long-folded piece of paper that might fall apart. She needed medical attention; she needed to keep still; she needed someone to look after Robin. She must see if there was anyone nearby who could help. Of course they would help. This was a genuine emergency with blood and danger — of course they would help. Her eyes filled with tears.

Timidly she got up and raked through the bedside drawers for a pad. She was overjoyed to find a crumpled sanitary towel, and once it was in place she felt so much better she walked confidently round the bed to the telephone. The doctor was out but his receptionist was kind and sympathetic which made her want to cry again. Now that help had been summoned she felt much better. Heartened, she rang Mrs. McAuley next door to see if she could help with Robbie.

The phone rang out for a long time and she was nearly

giving up when a sleepy young voice answered. It was Tracy, and she said her mother wouldn't be back before lunch.

"It's a coffee morning for the Red Cross," she explained.

"I wonder if you could help me, then —" Hester began.

"I dunno," said Tracy rapidly, "I'm studying today."

Hester wondered what she was studying in bed at 10a.m. — the blasted child had always been lazy.

"I'm sorry. I wouldn't bother you if it wasn't really urgent. You see I've started to bleed and I've sent for the doctor, but I should go to bed only I've got to think of Robbie. I can't lift him — or anything."

"What do you want me to do?" asked the girl, heavily.

Hester felt a moment of sympathy. At that age she would have been just as reluctant to be around sick people.

"Do you think you could come round and just — stand by. I'm going to ring James, but until he can get here Robbie needs someone to look out for him."

Tracy sighed.

"Oh, come *on*," thought Hester.

"I'll be a few moments — I'm not dressed yet."

"Studying, my eye," mumbled Hester as she hung up.

Robin came out of his room. She heard him breathing heavily as he crossed the landing in a laborious crawl. As he came thudding round the bed she avoided his eyes, but he was not to be put off. Inexorably he pulled himself to his feet and held out his arms.

"Up!" he instructed her.

She didn't know what to do. It wasn't that she didn't want him near her. More than anything she wanted to lift him onto the bed and lie curled round him, but lifting was out of the question.

"Come on, Robbie," she said carefully standing up, "we'll have to go downstairs to let Tracy in. You like

Tracy don't you?"

He may well have done so for he grabbed one of her fingers and they made very slow progress out of the bedroom — she holding herself together like a cracked egg — he swinging from her finger, bandy-legged and biting his fist. Halfway to the door she remembered that she hadn't rung James. To go back now would bring on Robbie's rage.

"Perhaps it will be better to wait until the doctor's been," she consoled herself. "It may be nothing and it would give him such a fright."

The voyage downstairs took for ever. Robin wasn't quite sure how to tackle them. He could crawl up them fast enough but down was still a problem and Hester held her breath at every step. Once he stumbled and swung his whole weight out into space on Hester's finger. She went cold with fear and felt her heart shrink inside her. She sat down on the stair in case she should faint and clung to him.

Looking down into the hall she wished passionately that the closed doors to the kitchen and the living room led to other places. She wanted to open them and find a completely new scene beyond where her life would be free of all these distresses and discomforts. It seemed almost spiteful the way that whenenver she had got things organised and she thought that now, finally, she would be allowed to enjoy life, something would go wrong. She crept onward down the stairs.

In the sitting room she found that things were still out of place from the night before. A magazine lay under a chair and coffee cups still sat on the coffee table. And James had left one of his little heaps of change on the mantlepiece.

"It'll never be straight again," she thought and tears stung once more.

The doorbell rang and she hurried to answer it. Hot

fluid ran out of her and she drew her breath in sharply. Tracy stood on the doorstep making it clear she was making a sacrifice. She walked past Hester without looking at her and sat down beside the baby. Hes dithered in the doorway then sat down again. She felt shivery. The windows of the living room squinted towards the sea and the room only caught the sun in the evening. Down the hill the houses were bright in the sunlight, and the dim green room seemed cold.

"Could you put the fire on please — I don't want to bend down."

"Okay."

Tracy did it quickly and sat down again.

"When will the doctor be here?" she asked.

"His receptionist couldn't say. With this practice he could be miles away!"

Just then the doctor's car appeared outside the garden. Tracy looked at Hester satirically.

"I'll go and let him in," she said with uneccessary emphasis. "You have to keep still."

The doctor strode into the room swinging his bag at the end of his arm as if he had just found it in the street.

"You should be in bed," he told Hester. She caught Tracy's eye.

"I was just going," she said

"Is your husband coming?"

"I don't know. I haven't rung him yet. I was waiting to hear what you'ld have to say."

He drew his breath in and blew it out eloquently through his moustache.

"My dear girl, any bleeding during pregnancy is a cause for concern. Could you please phone him now and get him here as soon as possible."

"I'll do that," said Tracy, impressed enough to make a contribution.

Hester allowed the doctor to help her up to the

bedroom where he laid her gently on the bed. She made a big effort and unclamped her thighs to let him take off her tights. The intimacy of the gesture made her even more tense and she could barely answer "have you fallen?" "have you any pain?" "is this the first time?" with a shake of the head.

"If you could open as wide as possible — " he said.

"Just like the dentist," she thought with a wild desire to snigger.

Blank faced he looked at her crotch.

"No pain at all," he repeated.

"None. The first I knew of it was when I went to the loo this morning."

"I see. Well, I'm not going to examine you internally myself in case I do more damage. I'll leave that to the boys at the hospital. It isn't severe, but we can't be too careful. I'll go and arrange your admission now. Just you lie still and don't worry."

As he left he remembered to try for a smile, and then she was alone, staring at the ceiling, while her stomach turned to iced water. Knowledge dawned slowly.

"Of course — I'll have to go to hospital. I should have thought of that. Oh God. They'll have to check it out. How will they manage without me? Poor wee Robbie! His mummy going away without warning."

In spite of the sunshine pouring in through the bedroom window, she shivered.

"That must be shock," she thought, "He shouldn't have left me alone like this. He can't be very experienced. He's new to the practice. He may be going thin on top and the moustache puts a few years on him but he can't be more than thirty."

Time dragged on. She felt petulant and forlorn.

"He really shouldn't have left me alone," she thought again.

She was alone with fear. She was steeped in it. Every

cell in her body was swollen with dread. It was spreading from this moment to all the other moments in her life, tainting the past and polluting the future — trickling outward and spreading like an incoming tide through sand. Nothing would ever be the same again, not now that she had found that disaster could really happen to her. The world was revealed as a cruel and chaotic place.

She lay in a side-ward of the obstetric wing of the area General Hospital. She was bored. At this point in the day — mid afternoon — the newly delivered mothers all around her were in bed and the babies were in the nursery. There was nothing to watch, and as she had been confined to bed since her admission that morning she couldn't go and find amusement. She was feeling much better, though, since she had seen the obstetrician. He had examined her gently but had not reached inside. He told her he thought she had a low placenta which could lead to a bit of bleeding in the last few months of pregnancy but it need not be a serious threat to her or the baby. Tomorrow she would have an ultra-sonic scan which would tell them more. If the scan confirmed his opinion she might be allowed to go hime, provided that she would spend as much time off her feet as possible, and "lift nothing heavier than a tea-cup." This had all cheered her immensely. Mr. Stewart was white-haired and energetic and she felt she could trust him.

However, until the scan was carried out and the acceptable truth confirmed she was confined to bed. Lunch had proved to be a waste of anticipation — limp chips, curly hamburger and cool baked beans, followed by something yellow floating in milk. She had been given a couple of crumbling magazines, but they were nonsense. Since she wasn't in the habit of reading in public she had no books with her.

The quiet soaked up any sound. She turned carefully

onto her side and looked out of the window. The day had been showery, but now the clouds had broken up and she looked out on scoured, rinsed and polished sky. The clouds had settled into two levels. At the lower there were some straggly grey bits and beyond and above them huge masses of strato-cumulus towered into the sky. The kind of clouds, she thought, that you could quarry salt or marble, or soap-suds, or shaving foam, or white lace out of...or pear blossom on a spring day, or seagull feathers. She was digging in her mind so deeply that she didn't hear the door open, and it wasn't until a husky voice spoke to her that she realised someone had come in.

"It's a grand day," said the other.

Hester turned, and saw a small dark woman sitting in the chair beside her bed.

"It is lovely now," she replied automatically, staring at her visitors. She had red-brown hair scraped back and parted in the middle; the eyebrows over her bulging eyes had been shaved; her skin was tanned and freckles clustered untidily on her long nose. Hester's gaze travelled below her receding chin to see that she was wearing a coat of short reddish-brown fur over her nightie instead of a dressing gown. The woman studied her calmly in return. She enquired,

"Ye widnae hiv such a thing as a spare cigarette on you?"

"I'm afraid I don't smoke."

"Ah didnae think ye wid when I saw ye."

The little woman fell silent and went on looking at Hester complacently as if she had just laid a golden egg.

"Yiv no had yir wean?"

"Not yet. I'm in for observation."

"Oh, aye. Ah've had mines, but they took it upstairs."

She pointed with her thumb at the ceiling to indicate the paediatric ward.

"Is your baby ill?" asked Hester sympathetically.

The woman nodded hard twice, paused and nodded again then fell silent and stared at the floor. Hes was sorry she'd asked. She made an effort to be sociable.

"What's your name?"

The woman lifted her head and gazed blindly out of the window.

"I am Mrs. MacCrimmond and my sons will be great pipers."

There came a rattle of wheels outside the door and she stood up hastily.

"I'll see ye again," she said and left.

A moment after a ward-maid come to tell Hester she had visitors.

"Who was that woman?" asked Hester.

"Who's that?"

"That little woman who just left here. She was wearing a fur coat over her nightie."

"Ach that one — I didnae see her come out. She's always up to something. Was she annoying you?"

"She didn't annoy me. She seemed a bit strange, but she only asked for a cigarette. She said her name was MacCrimmond."

"Her name's never MacCrimmond. She's just a tinker body. She gave you that name to keep out of trouble."

"Out of trouble?"

"Aye, they took her baby upstairs. Sister won't say why but I reckon it wis because she's an unfit mother. It could be because the wean's no right of course. Myra said they took her as soon as she was born — a' bundled up. Now she's got nothin' to dae but wander around and bother the other patients. I'll see tae her, don't you worry."

"She doesn't worry me. Please don't say anything to her on my account. I think she's got enough on her plate."

"We cannae have her pestering you when you're stuck in bed. You need your rest. I'll tell sister."

The thought of sister bearing down in wrath on the little woman was too much. Hester changed the subject.

"Who is it who's come to see me?"

"Ooh, here — I nearly forgot," said the woman unabashed, and trotted off.

Soon Hester's mother was sitting on her left, her sister on her right, and at the foot of the bed stood James, pulling at a stray hair in his moustache and shifting from foot to foot. He was no more at ease with his in-laws than Hester was with hers. Indeed, their self-assurance almost swamped him, especially when they were both together, and Hester had to keep making openings for him to enter into the conversation. She wished he could be clever and masterful as he was when they were alone, but he just stood, saying as little as possible and looking doleful, as now.

The hospital gown Hes had received on admission had no buttons at the neck. A nurse had stuck it together with tape but it had come apart again and she had to hold it together with her hand.

"I thought you would at least have your own good nightie with you," was her mother's opening comment.

"James packed a nightie for me ," said Hester defensively, "but they said not to wear it in case I get it all bloody — anything can happen." she added with relish.

"I'm sure it won't come to that."

"Catastrophic bleeding hasn't been ruled out," said Hester smugly.

Her mother didn't blink.

"I'm sure your hæmorrhage isn't that bad, dear."

"It's not a hæmorrhage, mother. A hæmorrhage is due to a ruptured blood vessel. You should know that."

Her mother ignored this just as she had always ignored her children when they had been rude in front of guests. Hes was sure she had struck home.

"Do you have everything you need?" asked her

mother.

"Yes, thank you, everything. There'd be no point in bringing anything else in, anyway. I will probably be getting home in a day or two."

Charlotte shook her head at her.

"C'mon, Hes, you can't have it both ways. Either you're going to bleed to death or you'll be home in a couple of days. Which?"

"The situation is this," said Hester, loftily, " — tomorrow I will go for an ultrasonic scan to determine the position of the placenta. Once they have that information they will know what to do. Until then no-one can be sure what will happen."

"That doesn't sound right to me," said her mother, flushing. "I've never heard of anyone with bleeding...like that being allowed out of bed, let alone out of the hospital."

"You don't have to believe me. You can ask sister. Mr. Stewart says that as long as I am never left alone and I spend all day in a chair I could be allowed home."

She leaned back and pulled the sheet up to her chin while mother and sister discussed this over the bed. At least James looked a bit brighter. She caught his eye and gave him a small secret nod. He smiled back and nodded. She knew she could depend on him to get her out of there come hell or high water and she felt brave.

We took a good look at mother and sister as they yakked about it.

The Family have got it wrong. Charlotte is usually written up as her father's daughter because she has the same sort of looks — auburn hair, brown eyes, yellow skin. Hes is 'Helen's double', as they say, for the same reason. This is all crap. Helen and Charlotte are two of a kind. They're what's known as 'good managers'. This is a way of saying they both get their jollies telling other people what to do. If the world was perfect and no-one needed organising they would die of boredom. If it wasn't for the fact they think politics is a dirty business they would be at it like a shot — two shots — running round asking people their grievances — promising to do something about them and maybe even doing it. Pressing the flesh — scoring off their opponents — and their colleagues — in politics it's all one — they would be happy as pigs in shit.

Hes's dad though — that was different. His idea of a good time was mooning round his fish-tanks all day — sometimes taking notes — sometimes just mooning. Or sitting with his books. It used to drive Helen nuts when he went off to his lab at the weekend. She never quite got round to asking him if he preferred his fish to her — she might have got the wrong answer.

Helen and Charlotte had finished their tête-à-tête and turned to nod at her.

"I'm sure we can manage it," said her mother smiling flatly at James, " — if you're agreeable, of course."

"Naturally," he said, agreeable to anything so long as he didn't have to discuss it.

"What?" rapped Hester. "What's going on, now."

"If you're to be allowed home, and I stress the if, James can be with you for the first two weeks. After that my term will be over and I can come and stay with you till August — I have no holiday booked — during the week, that is. After that Charlotte can cover the time."

You see what I mean?!

"What about James?" asked Hester, feebly. "He was going to take his summer holiday at the end of September as paternity leave."

"We'll all have to be flexible, dear, now that this has happened — including yourself."

"So, what if I have to stay in hospital until I'm delivered?"

"Well, much the same of course. James can come and stay with me if he likes, or he can cope with Robbie on his own for two weeks." Her tone said she didn't think he could. "Then I can take over when teaching stops." She frowned at Hester for being obtuse.

Slowly enlightenment came.

"You had all that planned already — before you even got to the hospital," cried Hester.

"Naturally. We had to draw up contingency plans when James rang. We weren't to know you could be getting out again."

There was no mistaking the accusation in her voice. Hester subsided into her pillows — she had been betrayed. No-one shared her vision, her faith in the goodness of her life. It was destructive to plan for the worst like that, for it might come true. She wouldn't have been surprised to find they had been sewing a shroud for her. Her eyes filled with tears.

"I'm sorry to spoil your nice plans," she said

"Oh, for God's sake, Hes!" snapped Charlotte. She hated emotional scenes.

"Don't call me Hes," said Hester in a strangled voice. "I know you hated it when I said you must stop calling me — my real name — you said so often enough. If you can't call me Hester at least call me — Hesione."

Charlotte shrugged,

"I don't give a shit what you're called."

Hester saw her mother giving her a 'don't-make-waves' look, of which Charlotte had had many. Now, as always, she ignored it.

"It's the truth. I was upset when you stopped using the name daddy gave you. It was rejecting his memory somehow. But now I understand, and I don't mind."

"Thanks a lot," said Hester.

"No, really. It's like this — Hesione, the character you were named after, was given a very hard time by her father — offered to the sea-monster and so on — so when daddy got killed you felt he had betrayed you and you rejected him and the name he gave you." The student of human nature finished her analysis.

Unnoticed by the others James had pulled one of the hairs out of his moustache and made his eyes water. To suppress a snigger Hester turned on Charlotte.

"You surely don't believe all that, do you? I thought you said you were a behaviourist — don't believe what you can't see and all that. It was just that all the other girls in my class had names like Ruth and Catherine and Janet, and I wanted to be the same. Children don't like to be different at that age, do they, mother?"

"No, they don't. They just want to be one of the gang. You were the same yourself, Charlotte."

Charlotte obviously was not pleased to be reminded that at one time she was one of the crowd, but she said nothing.

Helen stood up.

"I think we ought to be going. You need your rest." She shook out her coat, snapped her handbag under her arm and headed for the door. "We'll see you outside in a minute, James."

Charlotte followed her and James dutifully came round to kiss Hester goodbye.

"Now my husband needs my mother's permission to kiss me," she thought.

"You'd better hurry and catch them," she said, to mark their independence. "Give Robbie a kiss from me."

Ignominiously she began to cry. He sat on the bed and took her hand.

"I hope you will get home soon." he said, "D'you really think you will?"

"I really think so. I feel fine apart from — I don't think they'll keep me in. They need the bed." She summoned up a bright smile. "Don't let sister catch you sitting on the bed or you'll be for it."

"I'll come and see you on my own this evening," he said, getting to his feet.

"That'll be lovely. And d'you think you could bring me something nice to eat. The food in here is all they said it would be."

He grinned and made for the door.

"Jamie," she stopped him and he turned to her with raised eyebrows. She smiled and blew him a kiss.

"You can call me whatever you like." '

"Be careful when you say that," he replied.

4

Dear me, I can see you delicately withdrawing, up centre, and off.

Hester was sitting in the recliner outside her French windows. It was very warm and sunny and the flowers around her seemed to be lit from within. Silence surrounded her. In that position she could not see any houses, but she could see the sea, a thin gold line, above the hedge. The only sign of life was a bird which bounced in the middle of the lawn, stopped, stared at her from the corner of its eye and jumped into the air.

She watched it as it flew across the garden, swung back over the hedge and dipped out of sight. Then it burst back into view and soared up over her head. She followed its flight and was surprised to catch sight of an enormous moon floating in the blue sky behind her. Pushing her head further over the back of the seat, she studied this strange object. The surface was not the usual, dusty white, but shone like a pale gold, polished plate. The surface rippled slightly and she realised it must be the effect of sunlight on water. The moon drifted closer as she watched and she could see that below the clear water there was gold sand ridged with the pattern left by a retreating tide.

The bird reappeared sitting at her left shoulder and spoke in her ear. It said "the inland sea" quietly as a thought. Now the moon was so close she could see elegant ivory shapes, like fish bones, partly buried in the sand. She wanted to reach up and lift them clear to see what the buried parts looked like. She could imagine that they would be gilded and have diamonds glittering discreetly in the crevices.

Abruptly the moon was too close. It was on the point of forcing itself down over her face to smother her. Her head had fallen too far back to lift it. As she began to cry out she caught the smell of the sea on the surface and she tried to push the thing away. She tried to beat it off with her arms, but they felt as heavy as if they had been stuffed with sand.

She woke up.

She was in the passenger seat of a car, and her head had fallen off the head-rest and was jammed beside it. Her own strangled shout must have wakened her. She lay where she was and tried to remember what she was doing asleep in a car.

In a moment it came back to her. It was nearly the last day of the school term and her mother had wanted to collect things before the close. Hester had been made to swear a terrible oath that she wouldn't have any 'problems' while they were away, and Helen had packed daughter and grandson into her Fiat for a change of air in Glasgow.

The air, which had been hot and wet at the coast, was suffocating in the city. Trapped in the car, Hester felt like a chicken roasting in foil; the sanitary dressings she was obliged to wear constantly had chafed the inside of her thighs; the baby inside had grown enough to cheat her lungs of air. The doctors had discharged her on the understanding that she would do nothing but visit the doctor twice a week and come back the minute she lost any blood. This meant that she had nothing to do but watch her body for signs of deterioration, and fly into a panic from time to time when she became convinced that her heavy vaginal secretions were blood.

She was to spend the whole summer like a bead on a string sliding from husband to mother to doctor to husband... She was a parcel being passed around as in the game, only she was getting bigger and the music wouldn't stop. Once she had started to wash the ornaments from the bedroom and James had swept her off her feet into an armchair; her mother had snatched dusters off her with a rebuke about the unborn; the doctors smiled and nodded in imbecile content at her continued health, but they wouldn't tell her what it was that defined her as healthy so that she could enjoy it with them.

Now she was beginning to suspect that between them James and her mother were doing a better job of running the house than herself. It was silly to think like that, but James had re-organised the food in the deep-freeze by date rather than type, and when he explained it it seemed to make more sense. With her mother organising the time there were no tantrums, or even moments of doubt, from Robbie. Hester was surplus to requirements.

She looked back at the baby strapped in his seat. He was asleep, his head lolling back, his mouth open and hair clinging to the sweat on his forehead. It occurred to her that one day he would be an old man snoring in his chair. Inevitably he would grow ugly and hairy and the sweat that lay in clear beads on his lip would become laden with the odour of ripe human; the soft round cheek would be covered with hard stubble. She shivered and looked away into the street.

The land at the side of the school had been vacant ever since she could remember. At midday the children used it for football and the earth was bare. A tiny breeze swirled dust and dirty crisp packets into the air. The street was waiting to fill with noise and children. Inside the school a door banged.

Two girls came across the playground, one of them pulling on a wool coat with a grubby fur collar.

"They only have one coat, and they wear it all year round," thought Hester. Sweat ran down her back and there was a sudden hot flood in her crutch that made her clench her teeth and grip her handbag.

She had always tried to avoid her mother's school. She wished her mother's crusading conscience would have slept long enough to allow her to choose a school with quiet, well-dressed children. Charlotte told her this dislike was jealousy of the time their mother spent with them, away from her own daughters. She had gone on to do her own bit for the disadvantaged by teaching social workers. Hester went on hating the school. The tenements surrounding it that stared at her with blank curtained windows, the fly-covered dog shit smeared along the pavement and the shops with metal shutters partly rolled down all added up to something to loathe.

The school bell hammered.

Children sprang out of the ground and bumped into the car, waking Robin.

"Can't they see there's someone in it?" Hester raged.

The little girls were smiling and pointing at the baby; he was confused at first and started to snuffle, but the children distracted him. Hester felt like an exhibit in a case, but she managed to smile at the girls who all fell in love with her. She tried to look as if she was searching for something in her handbag. From the conversation she could hear she gathered they were trying to decide who she might be. Then she heard one of them say,

"Here yir Granny, now," to Robin. She looked up and was astonished to see her mother approaching across the playground.

"How do they work it out," she wondered, " — it's almost uncanny."

After a last word to the children her mother got into the car and started the engine.

"Let's get away before rush-hour," she said, and Hester nodded violently. It was a relief to be on the move. Her mother didn't talk when she was driving in traffic so Hes looked out of the window. Their route took them through streets of boarded-up tenements and half-demolished houses waiting to be refurbished. Hester wondered where the occupants went while their homes were being improved. It was common knowledge that there was a shortage of housing in the city so they couldn't be in other flats. She thought perhaps that they had been dehydrated like loofahs and packed on shelves in warehouses for the duration. Perhaps they had been shrunk and put to live in shoe-boxes. At all events they would have to be filed very carefully in case they were restored too soon and had to be de-hydrated again. It would be a painful process.

They were on the motorway and turning west. Hester sighed and shook the hair off her sticky neck. Robin was awake but amused by the passing sights so she didn't have to attend to him.

"How are we?" asked her mother for the sixth time that day.

"I'm fine," replied Hester.

"No trouble at all?"

She would have to give her something to chew on.

"A couple of tiny contractions — nothing more."

"Oh dear," said Helen in that sing-song intended to show that she wasn't worried so Hester shouldn't be either.

Hester smiled secretly. She knew what was expected of her. Life had to be kept smooth and pleasant and unpleasant facts ignored. "We'll cross that bridge when we come to it" was her customary response to a forecast of trouble, then she would spend as much time as possible dawdling about on the river bank until the crisis had passed. Now that a full-blown crisis had come upon her she might have to change some of her ways, but that would not include saying what was on her mind — least of all to her mother.

"Have you been in touch with Charlotte?" asked Helen.

"I told you — I rang her last Sunday."

"How did you find her?"

"Okay. She was tired — she always is at this time of year — exams to mark and so on. Why are you asking?"

"I was wondering — she didn't come over to see me this weekend."

"Oh?" Hester waited.

"It's this Frank. She never talks about him. There's no question of my ever meeting him — she's — I'm sure he's a bad influence. She's often been too late for lunch on Sunday, and a couple of times she's phoned to say she's ill — a hangover most likely — and won't be over at all."

"I'm sorry to hear that."

"He's always there when I ring. He answered once — he sounds very — I don't know. She never used to drink."

Hester was silent. They had both secretly tried alcohol when they were young — herself to see how much she could take without getting drunk; Charlotte to get drunk. As an undergraduate her sister seemed about par for her group, getting smashed a couple of times a term. Once or twice Hester had had to let her in. She was beginning to regret her complicity.

"I said she never used to drink," her mother insisted.

"Oh, it's just a phase, I'm sure."

"It's a phase she wouldn't have passed into by herself."

"You can't say that."

"She's my daughter."

"Mmmmm...?"

Hes recalled her agony one evening when her mother and father were going out with friends to a dinner. Her mother was wearing a gown of black velvet that looked stunning with her ash-blonde hair. The dress had only the thinnest of straps and one of them had slipped dangerously off her shoulder. Helen was swaying and laughing. She had raised her arms above her head and started to dance mockingly in front of her husband. Hester was stricken to see the other strap break and was sure the dress was going to fall. She had run to her mother's room to fetch a shawl but she wouldn't take it. Vainly, the miserable child had waited for a chance to drop it over the expanse of shoulder and bosom her mother was exposing to the world. As they left her father smiled at her and took the shawl with them.

"Don't worry about Char. She'll get over it — and him."

Her mother returned to the fray.

"D'you think she could take over from me for a couple of weeks in July? It might do her good to get away."

"Well...of course. If she wants to come I'll be glad to see her, but I thought you were all set to stay till the end of August."

"You'll have to let me have some time to myself," said her mother, irritably.

"Yes, of course," replied Hes thinking —

"So now I'm to be some kind of stalking horse for my sister! Cart her off to commuterland to let her see what's missing from her life. A nice house, a nice husband, a nice baby — and whammo — instant conversion to the great verities. I didn't know Ma could be so dense. As far as the old family are concerned Charlotte's the harlot and damned for good. Their intelligence services are red-hot. Well, they've got nothing better to do — Ma has.

"I've let the side down myself. Our family are supposed to breed with discretion, not go making spectacles of ourselves. Placenta Prævia, by God! What a shocker."

They had reached the countryside at last. For a while trees clustered thick beside the road which dipped and curved then at last she saw the sea shimmering faintly at the end of the tree tunnel. A narrow pavement ran beside the road and along it a woman was pushing a very tall, very old baby carriage. Something about the small figure in the white raincoat must have been familiar because Hester felt compelled to turn and look at her face as they passed.

It was Mrs. MacCrimmond. The protruding eyes, the chinless face, the red-brown hair were all the same. The difference was in the expression on her face — steady and intelligent — when their eyes met.

"She recognised me," thought Hester straining in her seat-belt to see more of the little woman.

With a gesture at once invitation and dismissal she raised her hand from the handle of the pram and pointed toward the golden sheet of the sea.

"Is there something wrong," her mother asked.

"It's a woman who was in the hospital with me. She had trouble with her baby."

"D'you want to stop and talk to her?"

"Heavens, no. The staff said she was a tinker."

"I hope I brought you up better than to turn your back on someone for a reason like that!"

"I don't mean that. She annoyed the staff, but she didn't bother me. I didn't think she was a tinker. And I'm sure she doesn't need my charity."

That night she woke sharply from a deep sleep. She lay still trying to find out what had wakened her. At first she thought it must have been Robbie and she listened for him but no sound came from his room. After a while she became convinced that what had disturbed her came from downstairs. A burglar? But the back of her mind answered no. How could she be sure? She didn't know, but she was sure.

She sat up slowly not to disturb James.

"It must have been mother," she thought, but she knew it wasn't.

She listened, turning her head to scan the air for anything — the faintest whisper — nothing. Holding her breath she slid out of bed and into her slippers and dressing gown. James stirred, but he didn't waken as she opened the door and stepped out onto the landing. She started for the stairs letting her breath wash soundlessly in and out of her open mouth as she passed the other doors.

Halfway down the stair one of her slippers fell off, bounded down several steps and stopped in the light from the front door window. Then she stopped and grabbed the banister as she realised at last why she had wakened. She didn't hear the slipper fall; she didn't hear anything. She could see everything, but she could hear nothing. A silence like the ocean floor surrounded her.

Fear was melting her and she lowered herself shakily to sit on the stair before her legs gave way.

"What has happened?" she wondered, shaking her head. No sound, "Brain damage? Pregnant women have strokes sometimes. My blood-pressure's been okay, though."

Panic, never far away these days, began to nitter at the back of her mind. She checked herself savagely.

"Go back upstairs right now and tell James. That'll help.

The sight of a friendly face is all you need to put this into perspective."

She started to get to her feet then stopped. She had seen something new. The fear she was dealing with made her slow and confused but piece by piece her seething mind put the picture together. The hallway of the house was L-shaped. The front door faced the foot of the stairs, the kitchen door was at the back of the hall and the door to the living-room was in the wall opposite the stairs. But tonight, in the wall beside the living-room door, another doorway had appeared.

The new door was of the same construction as the others, but it stood slightly open and through it Hester could see a wall, not built of brick like the rest of the house, but of rough stone. The wall was lit by a flickering light like that from a fire or a large taper and as she watched a thread of black smoke blew across it to disperse in the air of the hall.

Somehow she was sure the passage beyond led straight to the sea.

She became aware that she had wrapped her arms about herself and that she was moaning. Her lower lip was caught between her teeth and she could feel it vibrating with the noise she was making, although she still could not hear. It was essential that she should do something about the door, for until she did it would be equally dangerous open or closed. For the time being all she could do was sit here on the stairs and make sure that no-one went through it by mistake.

The sound of her moans had disturbed James's sleep. He woke at last, thinking that the baby was having a bad night, till he saw the bed was empty, then he jumped up in panic. From the bedroom door he saw her sitting huddled on the stair and shouted her name. She didn't seem to hear him, but he heard a sound from Robbie's room and cursed. He crept down to Hester and shook her shoulder.

She looked at him for a moment with no recognition, then something snapped and flew apart and she could hear once again. With a sob she flung her arms round his neck and clung to him. He half carried her into the bedroom and closed the door, not realising that she was trying to stop him from going downstairs.

"What's the matter with you?" he demanded. "Have you a pain? Are you bleeding again?"

She shook her head furiously trying to control her breathing. She pounded the mattress with her fist, pounded her thigh, her head, and finally she won. The sobbing stopped. She shook her head again to make sure of her hearing.

"No," she said at last, "there's nothing wrong — it was just a bad dream."

"What were you doing on the stairs? Did you walk in your sleep or what?"

"No, no. I thought I heard a sound and went to see. It was just a dream."

"You really should have wakened me. We can't have you wandering about in the night like that. Anything could happen."

Wearily she sat on the bed. At least the rest of the household had not been disturbed. As she kicked off her slipper she recalled the one still left lying on the stairs. For a moment she thought of asking James to go and get it for her, but the thought that he might see the doorway filled her with horror. It would wait till morning.

5

She gave me a good character, but said I could not swim.

That summer Hester and James took pains to spend the weekends together. The lack of privacy during the week made them conspirators for the first time in years as, when Mrs Paterson had left for the weekend, they planned their excursions like a pair of guilty children. On Saturday James would give the car a quick wash and see to any chores left about the house, but Sunday, even if it were raining, was for jaunts. They would avoid the town centre of Invergare as it was full of shuffling trippers dripping ice-cream, and head round the coast to find somewhere quiet.

One Sunday the rain held off and James announced that he would make a beach barbecue. They found a bit of shingle with some trees around it and James took Robbie to find firewood. Hester was left staring moodily at her legs and getting depressed. Low, thick clouds had reduced the hills across the loch to slag-heaps, and sea the colour of milky tea slopped ice-lolly sticks and sweetie papers onto the beach. Even perspiring was an effort.

She opened and closed pigeon-holes in her mind trying to find something pleasant to think about. She found she was rather short of that commodity and each time she passed thoughts stored under the heading "Not to be opened until..." they would slip out, fluttering and squawking, and have to be caught and crammed back in again.

Beside her on the rock she saw a patch of yellow lichen. The sight of it called up a vision of her father on the beach one afternoon. He was towering over her and telling her that from that yellow stuff it was possible to make a good red dye. She never questioned what he told her, even when it seemed improbable. He flung out one arm and addressed the sky.

"If you know what to look for you can find all you will ever need in or near the sea. Give me a hut on the beach and I will be content to live there for the rest of my life."

The thought that he would never know his idyll distressed her so she looked further afield for some amusement.

Among the rocks nearer the sea she saw a small pool. She decided to take a chance and walk over to it for the sake of the distraction it would afford. Lying on her side she could keep the light from the surface and see clearly into its depths. She was delighted to see anemones and shrimps among the weeds and settled down with her head on her arm to watch the activity. The pool was deeper than she would have thought from its position and far down she could see something stirring. All at once she realised she was looking at a pair of mobile black eyes.

"A crab!" she thought, and leaned closer.

Too close, as it turned out, for she overbalanced. Frightened of violent activity, she could not stop herself and slid right into the water. The pool was not large and she was surprised to find herself completely immersed. She was lying opposite the ledge where she had seen the eyes and saw now that they belonged to a hermit crab.

"What's he doing here?" she wondered, and the crab's answer came to her like a voice speaking into the bone behind her ear.

"Nothing doing," he snapped.

His body was hidden in a plump cowrie shell, festively hung with bright green streamers of weed. Apart from his button eyes and the tips of his claws none of him was visible, and the claws trailing below his shell made him seem to be standing on tiptoe.

"I'm sorry," she thought back. "I meant that I was surprised to see one of...your kind...here. It's not usual..."

"Willy Nilly. Waiting."

"Oh? What are you waiting for?"

"You, fool."

"Me? Why are you waiting for me?"

"Tardy are," he replied, and abruptly turned away and disappeared. She was left staring stupidly at the space where he had stood thinking —

"This is a dream. It has to be a dream. Crabs don't speak."

Suddenly he was in front of her again.

"Moveit!"

"Where?" she said, involuntarily copying his style.

"Here!" he said, and turned away again.

"Since this is a dream," she thought, "I may as well try and follow him. Anything can happen."

Sure enough, when she thrust herself towards the crevice she found she was following the crab down a tunnel. The walls were gloss-painted and rivetted to them was an entirely redundant hand-rail. The crab's thought anticipated her question.

"Manmade."

There was no mistaking the disgust in his tone. Hesione slithered after him steeped in mild curiosity until the tunnel ended. She wriggled out and found that they were on a ledge hung far above the bottom of the sea. There was a sound of chiming in her head and she wondered what caused it. The crab answered,

"Bell-tower," and pointed with a massive claw across the sea-bed. In the dimness she could make out a tall, white shape.

"Is that where I must go now?"

He said nothing but his claw still pointed so she slid off the ledge and floated away in the direction indicated. His thought followed her.

"Come straight home after school!"

Soaring high above the sea-bed, Hesione was giddy with delight. The water supported her like clear jelly, and she found movement through it as easy as walking — easier for one in her state.

"I wish I could always move like this," she thought.

As she approached the bell-tower she could see that the walls were covered with rounded white nacreous tiles like gigantic fish scales or mother-of-pearl sequins. At the top was a solid pink dome. Three oval windows appeared on the side nearest her, but she could see no sign of a door. All at once the wall was in front of her and beyond it she saw now that what she had taken to be merely rocky horizon was in fact a massive, jumbled city. The chiming in her head was getting louder. A green scaly face appeared at one of the windows.

"You'll have to hurry," it said in her mind. "You should have been there ages ago."

"Where do I have to go?" asked Hesione, and there

came a sigh of exasperation. A stream of bubbles appeared from the face.

Just then a cloud of gold-striped fish rose into view on the other side of the tower. They all had prim little mouths and solid dark eyes like those on an old china doll. It was a shoal of saupe. She watched them as they flashed towards her, then turned left, then right, then left again. All at once she was swimming in a soup of glittering bodies and she turned and swam with them, fairly sure they were going to the right place. Uneasy, she became aware that the solid little bodies were bumping into her, brushing her face, tangling in her hair and swimming inside her clothes. Soon there were several of them inside her shirt tickling her breasts. She forced herself to concentrate on keeping up with the shoal but the sensation was very disturbing and once she was nearly overwhelmed when she felt a tweak at her nipple. She was glad she was wearing tights.

Suddenly the shoal fell away beneath her. Below she could see an oval stadium built out of black stone. At either end there was an enormous television screen like an American football pitch and the banked seats seemed to be teeming with life. There were still more shoals to come, however, for she could see them making their erratic, shimmering way towards them.

She sank carefully toward the auditorium, and landed herself on one of the front benches. More and more fish piled in around her and the flashing of the bodies left her with the impression of a great din all around. Just as she was wondering when the teacher would appear the big television screens flickered into life. The words, "Good evening, children," appeared on them both. All around her visual silence fell as the fish became still and aligned themselves across the benches to keep one eye on each screen. Words began to march steadily across the screens saying,

"This evening we will be continuing our biology course, Element no. 4 — Land Surface Life Forms; Environmental Determinants of Metamorphosis."

Hesione felt panic.

"I'm going to need to breathe soon," she thought.

"If you need to leave the class," wrote the television smoothly, "be so kind as to raise your right flipper."

She raised her hand and the screen said,

"Follow the blue arrows to the pod-room."

A series of arrows appeared on the screen running from left to right, and following their movement she saw a gap in the bleachers which led to a cave. She swam into it, under an archway marked PINNIDAE and into a brightly lit chamber with tiled walls. There the vault of the roof rose clear of the water.

Aching with gratitude Hesione surfaced and hung gasping on a ledge which seemed designed for the purpose. Her heart burst into furious activity when oxygen hit her bloodstream and her whole body shook with its beating. As she waited for the thundering to subside she looked around her at the tiles and noted that they had been painted. She looked closely at the designs and found they were childish paintings of trees and flowers, and, commonest of all, humans. They were shown naked and with such crudely enlarged genitals that she blushed. Some of them were depicted in the middle of sexual intercourse. She tore her eyes off the drawings, emptied her lungs and plunged back down through the archway.

Back in the auditorium the screens were flickering away producing a machine-gun fire of information. She tried to pick up the sense of it but the vocabulary was obscure and she had missed most of the introduction. It was saying,

"Unlike the locust, however, the bipedal mammals do not evince such metamorphosis as a result of change in climatic conditions. We must conclude therefore that the invariance of form is phylogenetic..."

In no time at all she found her gaze wandering around the arena trying to identify the different species of fish. Only the occasional sentence caught her attention.

"— will suddenly erupt and destroy many adjacent cells as with our friends Meandrina, Astroides and Carphylla, the aggregate skeleton... ...Symbiotic or parasitic life-form assisting in the process..."

But it was no use. She could never concentrate on lectures like that. A school of slivery-white fish rose and swam to the centre of the arena, blushing pink as they went. The screen introduced them —

"Student body, Pelagic 372, has been on a field trip and have some interesting data to offer us."

Hesione wondered how they might communicate to a mass audience with no speech and was pleased to see them arrange themselves into strings that spelt out words. Nevertheless the lecture still made no sense to her and she decided to go and seek out the source of the television display. By wriggling gently she lifted out of her seat, feeling clumsy and conspicuous in the svelte, shiny crowd. To her horror she saw her own face appear on the screen, and her vast, bloated image gaped at her from both ends of the arena.

"Oh, my God," she thought, "I must be passing in front of a camera. Where is it?"

She tried to accelerate out of the shot, but it was of no avail, for every time she looked up she saw her pink, translucent face staring vacantly back at her. With a massive effort of will she soared up over the wall of the arena and away.

"How embarrassing," she thought. "I never liked school, but that was the worst ever."

She became aware of a voice calling her name. It

came, muffled and erratic, from the direction of the bell-tower. Languidly she rolled over in a long, banking turn and swept towards that edifice. She was beginning to enjoy the sensation of skill and strength in her body. The voice came again like a badly tuned radio, but there was some urgency in its tone. She floated to the surface. James was standing over her, nudging her with his foot.

"C'mon, Hes. Wakey, wakey, rise and shine."

She sat up and rubbed the sleep from her eyes.

"Sorry," she said, "I was watching the crab and dozed off."

James had collected a small heap of grass and tarry sticks which he persuaded to produce great quantities of smoke, but no heat. He had gone red in the face from blowing at it. Robin copied him and trundled round the fire blowing wetly. Wherever Hester sat the wind whimsically blew the smoke over her.

"I'm sorry, love," said James at last to her streaked face, "it looks as if it'll have to be squishy sardine sandwiches again. I'll never get the sausages cooked on that."

"Aye," she said, "and I'm going to get kippered."

James scooped up the baby.

"I'm going to make one last try for some wood up at the headland. If I don't find anything there I promise I'll give it up."

"I'm coming too," she said huskily and stood up.

"D'you think you should? The stones can be awfully slippy and you might — you know — if you fell and twisted yourself."

"If I stay here I'll cough myself into a miscarriage.

Besides, I've had enough lying around for today. Look, I'll stay up the beach, on the shingle. It'll be easy to walk there."

As they approached the headland by their seperate routes she began to have regrets. The shingle got deeper and looser as she went along and her feet were constantly slipping sideways and down. After some yards of this she had to stop and pant because she had unconsciously been holding her breath.

"This was a bad idea," she gasped.

She looked up to see where her men had got to. They seemed miles ahead, and she despaired of catching up with them. A clump of children stood on the black rocks of the headland, their skinny white legs weaving backwards and forwards as they poked at a humped shape on the tide-line. When James reached them they stopped prodding and talked to him animatedly, waving arms and sticks and pointing all over the beach. James nodded and pointed at the sea and the children ran off, their voices carrying to Hester like the cry of gulls.

She tried to call to James but the tide had turned and the sound of the sea against the rocks swamped her voice. The rocks running out to the headland from her position looked promisingly flat, so she took another determined breath and began to pick her way over them.

When at last she caught up with James she found she was stranded some six or eight feet higher than him. He still could not hear her as he was intently studying a rotting seal carcase. She stood looking down at him from the basalt slabs wondering how she could get to him. Fortunately Robin looked up and saw her and his excitement drew James's attention to her predicament.

"What are you doing up there?" he shouted,

"The shingle was loose so I came along the slabs."

"They must be slippery, aren't they?"

"Not just now — they're dry — but they'll be wet and

dangerous when the tide comes in. D'you think I can get down or shall I go back?"

"It's not very nice down here with that thing," he indicated the corpse with his foot. "It's mingin', as we used to say."

"You come up here, then. We can all go back this way."

"I can't leave this thing on the beach. It'll foul it up for swimmers. If I can move it down a bit I'm pretty sure the tide will lift it. I won't be long."

He started back along the beach to where he had seen a plank, but Robin was not happy at being separated from his mother again so soon and began to yell and hold his arms out to her with his fingers clutching the air.

"I'd better come down," she shouted.

"Okay — tell you what — sit down with your feet over the edge and drop. I can catch you — it's only a couple of feet that way."

"Seems a bit risky."

"It's that or grow wings."

The humidity was fraying his temper.

"Alright — be careful you don't hurt yourself. That would be too much."

She slid off the rock into his arms. He sagged a bit but held up.

"Look," he said, jouncing her, "I told you I could support the whole family."

"Put me down — you'll strain yourseslf."

"Not a chance," he grunted, but he wasted no time in lowering her to the ground.

"I mustn't be so daft in future. Think what could have happened."

They went to the carcase. The smell — an oily, rotting, sea-smelling reek of decomposition — made her gag but curiosity got the better of her finickyness and she approached it slowly.

The seal seemed to have been trying to get back to the

sea when it died. It lay, partly on its side, facing down the beach, its body arched and its head pulled back. The skin round the mouth had dried and shrunk so that the teeth were bared in a grin of agony. The eyeballs had been pecked out.

"The poor thing," said Hesione as James pushed at it with his foot.

"Look," he said, "the skin's all dried, so it must have been dead for a while, but the blood in the eye-socket looks fresh."

"That's because a seal's blood is redder than human's — it's thicker and got more red cells — no — myoglobin they call it. That holds more oxygen for them so that they can empty their lungs when they dive. "

"That figures — if they kept their lungs full they couldn't sink," said James the engineer.

"They can stay under water for more than twenty minutes at a time and their heart all but stops beating. Then all their blood fetches up in this huge blood vessel just in front of their heart — the anterior vena cava. A long time ago men used to use it for trousers."

"How d'you know all this?"

"Daddy must've told me."

"You should've been a vet."

"Don't be daft — I hate animals."

"People always identify with seals," he said, "but I can't see them as human knowing that about them. They're not like us at all. They're aliens on the same planet."

"Maybe. But then again, perhaps other humans are more alien than we think."

This thought made them both uneasy so James left Robbie beside her and fetched his plank. Sticky blackness fouled the sheen of the water-polished wood.

"What's that horrible stuff?" she asked.

"That? It's crude oil."

"But it's all lumps. I thought it was tar."

"Hester, people haven't used tar on ships for decades."

"Oh, no, of course not. How stupid of me. Is that what killed her?"

"Could be. Could've been a ship — could've been a salmon fisher."

He jammed the plank under the seal's shoulder.

"If I can turn her maybe I could roll her down the beach a bit."

"I wish he'd leave her alone," she thought. "We've no right to maul her around like this. We're strangers — we should show more respect and let the sea take her."

Suddenly she felt heat on the back of her head. She looked at the sky. The sun was still hidden by heavy cloud, but as she watched this changed from grey to white. She heard a crack and looked down to see James holding part of the plank. It had broken but the seal's muzzle had been turned and now it faced her as if in supplication. The sweet, oily smell hit her throat again. All at once the seaweed round her feet was hissing with white hopping things.

"Oh, leave it — leave it, please!" she shouted in desperation, and hot fluid ran out of her.

He stopped, looking cross.

"Please," she begged, "I think I'm bleeding — all this moving about."

At that he came to her quickly.

"Can you make it to the car?" he asked, his face pinched with worry.

"Yes — it's not sore. Only please hurry."

It was nothing, of course, but she had the impression he was as glad as she to have a reason to go back. All he said was,

"Better safe than sorry. Just don't frighten me like that again."

6

Thou debosht fish, thou.

That night she dreamed again that she awoke to silence. Without hesitation she put on her dressing gown and hurried downstairs. The door had appeared and straightaway she went and pushed it open.

The passage beyond the door was lit by tapers in rusty sconces and it curved to the right and down. The flagged floor was lightly strewn with fine white sand; the walls were of roughly worked stone and the roof was cut out of the living rock. She stepped down into the passage and her feet grinding on the sand sent tiny echoes spattering away from her.

"I can hear again," she said, and her voice moaned off along the tunnel and came rolling back. The sound frightened her but she said,

"I'm not going back until I've seen something."

For answer the door behind her shut with a clang that set the echoes tearing into the air about her. The din squeezed her head.

"Quiet!" she yelled, pressing her hands to her ears. "If you're not quiet I won't come."

At once the racket died down but as she started along the tunnel whispers clustered round her — tittering at the nape of her neck — hissing at her elbow — a hooting laugh at the small of her back nudging her on faster.

"I'm coming. I'm coming."

The echoes of her voice swept the whispers away and left her in silence for a moment. Then, as she walked along the passage she could hear voices from beyond the walls. Most were indistinct, but once she heard a shout — "Help, Johnny, help!" — and the sound of running feet. The whole area of the tunnel seemed densely inhabited by sounds — a baby's chuckle, a crash of falling metal as if someone had dropped a lot of cutlery — and other, unfamiliar sounds — lisping speech, the weeping of something not human, the roar of a distant explosion. She spoke to encourage herself,

"Well, this is something to tell my grandchildren," and again the sound of her voice brought a frightened, listening silence.

Downward and round she travelled in a long gentle spiral with tides of whispers washing about her. At last she rounded a curve and was not surprised to see Mrs MacCrimmond in her crumpled white raincoat. She held something in her hand and thrust it at Hesione in silence. It was a shell smeared with grey-brown paste and she pointed at it with a long clawed finger. Hesione poked at it with her finger and some of the stuff stuck to it. Mrs MacCrimmond pointed to her eyes. Hesione hesitated and sniffed at it. The smell reminded her of the dead seal and she was sickened. The other scrubbed at her own eyes, showing her what to do. With a slight shrug Hesione drew her finger over her eyelid.

For a moment nothing happened, then suddenly she was struck to her knees by pain. Blinded, and with tears pouring down her face, she tried to wipe the ointment off, but her hands were seized and her face pressed against the wall. The wall swung away from her and she stumbled forward and half ran, half fell, into an open space. Mrs MacCrimmond's voice followed her as she staggered away.

"You have until dawn."

Hesione stopped and swabbed at her eyes with her dressing-gown. At first she thought she was in darkness, but as her eyes dried she became aware of light. Carefully she sat down and waited.

"After all, my hearing came back," she told herself.

Her eyes stopped hurting at last and she began to see fuzzy shapes which got sharper as the seconds ticked by. Finally she could see where she was. She was sitting on the floor at the foot of a low bed where a woman lay on her back among tumbled white, bloodstained sheets. Her head was back and the sheets were pulled up to her chin so that Hesione couldn't see much, but from the lumpy shape under the sheet she guessed that the woman was pregnant.

It was no longer night in this place. The room was lit by a row of high windows through which she could see blue sky and clouds. The walls were bare, smooth sandstone. There was a heavy wooden door in the wall to her right and beside it there was a plain chair and an oak chest. Against the wall on the left there was a long trestle table where two women stood talking, their backs toward her, their voices an indistinct murmur. They wore long brown dresses and their heads were bound with white cloth like a loosely made turban. When one of them reached across the table Hesione saw that the hand had only four fingers with long, claw-like nails, and a slight webbing between. The absence of a thumb was the most frightening thing she had seen or heard. She watched intently to see if she had been mistaken, then one of the women turned and looked straight at her. Brown, bulging eyes in a chinless face studied her for a moment, then turned away with no sign of recognition. Hesione tried to speak, but her mouth would not open.

The woman on the bed moaned and one of the others went to her. She was wearing the same binding on her head, but now the other pulled it off letting a mass of red-brown hair loose onto the pillow. The woman moaned again and rolled her head and her sister took the hair and braided it swiftly round the wooden posts at the bed-head. Hesione was horrified.

"It will keep her still," the woman explained. "We always do it. You should be glad. You had better get busy — it's nearly time."

Hesione tried to ask what she was supposed to do, but all she could get out was a strained hum. The other woman came up behind her and took hold of both her hands.

"She's having her baby," she said in a loud, hooting voice, "and she needs help. Only a full human can help her at this stage."

She shoved Hesione against the end of the bed. Hes tried hard to speak to explain that she wasn't a midwife and knew nothing about delivering babies, but it was no use. She grew more frightened. The woman in labour moaned and moved. There came a wet, sucking sound. The woman who had bound the other's hair now took her hands and strapped them to the bed irons at her side. The woman holding Hesione forced her hands under the sheets. Hesione struggled but the little woman was too strong for her. The woman in bed screamed and moved and at once her hands were covered in hot brine-smelling fluid. Hesione found her voice and gave a strangled yell.

"Grab hold of it. Hold on! Hold on!" said her captor.

She clutched at something. It was slimy — appalling. The mother screamed and strained at her bonds. Hesione recalled drawing a chicken. She couldn't bear to look, but with her hands she traced the woman's stringy thighs to the groin and felt for the opening. The pudend was hairless and, as labour was well advanced, she found the opening easily. Both her hands slid in without obstruction and her captor at last let her free. The mother screamed again in pain, but she seemed to realise help was near for the scream was short. Hesione felt something being pushed against her hands. She took a firm hold and tugged enquiringly.

"Not yet!" shouted the woman at the bed-head, " —just hold onto it."

Hesione held it and waited. The woman in labour panted gently for a minute, then drew in a big breath and bore down. Her thumbs were nearly dislocated by the pressure and the slimy thing she held was nearly sucked back inside, but she clung on. It began to move toward her again.

"Pull now," yelled her companion.

She pulled gently and it slid faster and faster toward her until, with a roar from the mother, it slumped out onto the bed.

The helper pulled back the sheet and Hesione saw that the baby was covered in spotless white fur. This bewildered her, for she had blood up to her elbows and the bed was drenched with it. As she gazed into the beseeching eyes of the baby the blood started to drain over the edge of the bed like thick soup. One of the helpers brought a bowl from the table to catch it as it ran, and when it stopped running she scraped it off the bed with the side of her hand.

The other helper shook Hesione by the shoulder.

"What are you going to do about her?" she bawled.

"Do about whom?"

"The baby — it's yours now. You brought it into the world."

"What about...?"

"The mother?" The other shrugged her thin shoulders. "Placenta prævia — she's done for."

"Oh, no!" said Hesione, and tried to explain that the condition was not fatal but her mouth failed her again.

For answer the other pointed to the bed. Hesione saw that the body was already stiff, the back arched and the teeth bared in a last agony of pain. The skin was dark brown and drying so fast that, as she watched, the cuts on the wrist made when they had been strapped to the bed split, and the skin curled back. There was no blood.

"I'm sorry," said Hesione, "oh, God, I'm so sorry."

She pulled the baby towards her and, in spite of the smell of blood and decaying fish, she buried her face in the soft white fur.

"What else could I do?" she sobbed. "I'm sorry. I can't do anything for you."

All at once she started to fall. The bed and the baby melted away and her vision will filled with shining mist. She tumbled forward, head over heels, for what seemed like hours. Then, at last, she felt floor under her. She opened her eyes and found she was lying in front of the sitting-room fire.

She lay still for a while and listened happily to the sounds of her home — the clock ticking, the click and chunter from the fridge, a car passing on the distant main road.

She clambered to her feet, her limbs heavy with exhaustion, and opened the curtains. Dawn was reddening the sky to the east.

7

He made them, every one.

It was the middle Sunday of August and they went to visit James's parents. The day had been dark and long, trailing curtains of rain had dragged endlessly across the distant hills. Later in the afternoon, however, it was at least dry so the men took the baby to the allotment. Mrs Grieve busied herself in the kitchen. Hester was left in the living-room to watch television, but she had spent too much time doing that recently and could work up no enthusiasm for more. By and by she got up and lumbered through to the kitchen.

"Can I do anything to help?" she asked.

Her mother-in-law looked up, startled. It was a long time since she had made such an offer for she had so often been met with a polite refusal — "No, you just take it easy — this is my treat" — that she had given up. Taken thus aback Mrs Grieve did not send her away.

"Not at all. Just you sit down, my lass," she said, and when Hester still stood in the doorway she pulled a padded stool from under the small folding table.

"When Jim and I are alone we eat in here," she explained, blushing a little. She was sure Hester would think this unrefined. "It saves carrying everything."

"Mmm. We do that, too," said Hes, nodding.

She didn't tell her that this had only been since she had lost control of the household. She rested her elbows on the table and looked round while Mrs Grieve turned back to her work. For the first time Hes studied her mother-in-law. She was tall, though not as tall as herself, and had a big rectangular skeleton made of big rectangular bones. She was well covered, but nothing about her sagged, and she gave the impression of being firm, braced and ready for anything. Her iron-grey hair was neither too long nor too short and of the kind that knows how to keep its place; her actions as she sliced up a lump of corned beef were decisive and uncomplicated. Hester felt a pang of envy.

"I wish you'd let me do something. I'm not ill — only pregnant."

Mrs Grieve looked at her. Hester was aware that her own face looked puffy and unhealthy.

"You're needing more exercise," said Mrs Grieve.

"Aren't I just," she agreed.

"Never mind. It'll no be long now."

"It can't be too soon for me."

"Aye."

She turned away again and began to arrange the corned beef on a plate.

"How's your mother," she asked for the sake of form.

"She's fine. Glad to get away from me, though. She likes to get about more — so do I for that matter — but right now I'm stuck in the house and she's stuck with me."

"Aye," said Mrs Grieve, and that threatened to be the end of the conversation till suddenly she added,

"When I got married, just before the war, you didn't

go out at all once you were big. You didn't like to show yourself."

"How Victorian," exclaimed Hester warmly. "That really was a confinement."

"Aye, confinement's right. You didn't go out and you only saw your family and women friends — that was if you fancied yourself respectable. There was a lot of nonsense in those days."

Hester laughed, and Mrs G. was encouraged.

"D'you know," she continued, turning right round and resting her hip against the unit in a way that suggested long years of habit, "to this very day some of the older women round here won't praise a baby to its face — in case it gets carried off, I think. I'm no sure what they're frightened of, but they always call a baby bad names."

"I think that's true all over. I've never heard my mother call Robin anything but "That wee man" — come to think of it she's never said anything nice about me — but I think she'd have a fit if you said she did it to keep off the fairies."

"Aye, right," agreed her mother-in-law, drily. "Now tell me — d'you cut his fingernails?"

Hester raised her eyebrows in reply so she went on,

"My mother told me you were always to bite your baby's fingernails off and burn them in case they got into the wrong hands — she'd never say whose."

"D'you mean witches?"

"Something like that. Everybody's got a bit of super-stition in them somewhere. I mind once when James was in his pram — I left him outside the close while I took the shopping in — I came down to fetch him and there was this old woman standing over the pram. She was a mess I can tell you — white hairs all over her face and newspaper keeking out of her shoes — well, I was going to see her off, but Mrs Armstrong — she lived in the ground floor house in those days — she came barging out of the close, and she was raging! She chased the poor old soul — and the language! — then before I knew what was happening she came over and scratched Jamie's poor wee lip till it bled. Just there, under his nose."

"That's terrible," said Hester, shuddering. The thought of James as a baby in pain brought tears to her eyes.

"I was wild, of course." Mrs Grieve went on. "'Whit ye dae that for?!' I says. 'Oh,' she says, calm as you like, 'that old woman's got the evil eye.' She was a country body herself. 'How'd you go an' scratch the wean like that?' I says. 'That'll keep him safe,' she says. 'You always dae that.'

"Jamie was yelling his head off, so I couldnae really get talking to her about it, but I was mad. So was Jim, but, ach, she didnae mean any harm. We asked some other old yins about it and they said it was right enough. My mammy said we should have made a sign of the cross over him as well — and her a good Protestant too! My dad said we should have smeared the pram wi'...something else...he could be awful coarse could my father."

She turned back to her work and fell silent for a moment while she stripped the skin from a spring onion. Then, looking up thoughtfully, she said,

"Ach it was a lot of nonsense, but it kept people happy, I suppose. People get feared when times are hard and they need their notions — and, my God, times were hard."

She shrugged.

"Tell you what you could do for me. Could you go and get the tray from the room? It should be down beside the table."

"Gladly," said Hester, getting to her feet carefully in the tiny space. In the living-room she stopped and looked round. She took in the rough textured walls, the brown tiled fireplace filled for the summer with dried flowers, the fitted carpet and the shell-framed pictures that

James's sister had brought from her honey-moon in Spain. The lamp on the television threw a generous, warm light over the room in contrast to the darkness of the day outside.

"I like it here," she thought, "it's clean and comfortable and tidy. What more could anyone want?"

She took the tray to Mrs Grieve who opened a cupboard and took out crockery saying,

"Are you alright with cheese? I couldnae stand it when I was carrying Jamie."

"I'm fine with cheese." Hes replied and added, "I never have any fads. It might be better for my waistline if I did."

"Nonsense — you've got to keep your strength up," then, "See that lettuce beside the sink? D'you think you could give it a wash? You can sit down to do it."

Delighted to be accepted in this manner, Hes pulled the chair over and turned on the tap.

"I warn you," said Mrs Grieve, "It'll be hoaching wi' things. Jim grows them at the allotment, but he will not put plastic down — says he likes the soil to breathe — and the slugs get into them."

Hes put the lettuce under the tap and turned the water up to full pressure. Her mother-in-law sliced tomatoes and said,

"Course it would be grand if they were like the ones from the supermarket — all done up in polythene and no' a beastie in sight — but it's no' what you'd call a hardship to wash a lettuce."

Hester laughed nervously and Mrs Grieve joined her cheerfully. For the first time she thought her daughter-in-law wasn't such a bad lassie.

"We don't know we're born, nowadays, really," she went on. "My mammy never had a vacuum cleaner in her life — never expected to have one — she brushed all her carpets — no that we had that many — just rugs."

Hester turned from the sink to answer her and they spent some moments on the disadvantages of a linoleum surround. When she turned back to the sink she saw something had been washed out of the lettuce and a roaring filled her ears. Two pinkish brown slugs and a small red worm were tumbling about among the swirls of grit. The worm lashed about but the slugs lay supine and mute. Hes lifted the lettuce between the tips of her fingers, picked the leaves off one by one and held them under the tap. A colander had appeared on the draining board and she dropped the leaves into it hoping they were clean. She couldn't bring herself to look closely at them. At last she reached the heart and broke the last, pale leaves off the slug-eaten stem.

Then, with sinking heart, she turned her attention to the contents of the sink. Lifting out the discarded leaves she found that the worm had nearly been swept down the drain, but was still flailing gallantly. The slugs had doubled in number and seemed to have doubled in size and all but one lay right side up and was heading up the side of sink. With an agonised shudder Hes turned the rubber spout of the tap on them all and washed them down the drain. The inert one approached the hole last, and as it began to move it arched itself in a last gesture of yearning before it plunged into the blackness. She let the water run to make sure they were well away, but as she thought of them smothering in the darkness of the drain, fighting for air, blind and drowning in the falling water, she was smitten with guilt.

"After all," she thought, "they only wanted to live. Just like any other creature."

A wave of grief swept over her. She leaned her arms on the sink, dropped her head on them and began to cry.

"I'm sorry," she whispered, "I'm so sorry. I couldn't help it. I'll try not to do it again."

She heard a sigh from Mrs Grieve, then she was pulled round to press her face against the older woman's firmly packed body. She threw her arms round her and sobbed aloud.

"Poor wee girl," Mrs Grieve said, and continued with soothing phrases like — "you've got a lot to put up with right now. It's no easy. Don't you worry — you'll be alright — they can do wonders nowadays."

Locked together they swayed gently until the storm passed, then Hester, embarrassed and gratified, pulled away to blow her nose.

"Thank you, I'll be alright, now, I'm sure." she said, but ten minutes later when James appeared at the kitchen door she was still pink and shaking. He was surprised to find her in there with his mother and was astounded when the two of them looked at the baby, giggled and chased him out again.

"Go and get that wean clean," his mother ordered, "just look at the states of him. Gardening was it? Coal-mining, more like."

And Hester said,

"Men — they've no idea. They'll let kids get into anything."

8

...like this insubstantial pageant faded.

Hesione stood with her suitcase at her feet. It was the end of September, the long summer was past, and it was time for her to go to hospital and deliver the baby. Already the grass was yellowing; shadows in the morning were getting longer; spider's webs were heavy with water drops; roses were fat and brown and rotted in the early frost.

"Time is up for the roses and for me," she thought, "We must both drop this swelling we've been growing over the summer. All summer I've been sitting still and swelling like a flower that rotted in the bud. This is not a 'joyful event' it's just a sloughing off."

She sighed and turned to wave to Robbie. He was being held up at the sitting-room window in the arms of Tracy and was still in his pyjamas. James had changed his nappy but she wished she could have left him ready for the day, at least.

James backed the car out into a cloud of steam and beckoned her in through the hazy window. Everybody was on the other side of glass. She slid carefully into the car while he put her suitcase in the boot.

"Cheer up," he said, "it's nearly over now."

She tried to smile for him but as they drove off she could only think of the hectic, happy preparations they had made for Robin. It had been like Christmas with all the gifts for one person, nappies and baby-gros and vests — a cot and a pram — and painting his room. In any case there would not have been so much to do for this baby, but it would have been nice to buy something new for her. She sighed.

"You're not too worried, are you?" said James. "It'll be alright."

"I'm not worried. It's just such an anti-climax — all those weeks waiting for something bad to happen — never quite sure if I was going to take her to term — now here we are, calm as you please, and I'm not even in labour."

"Don't tell me you'd rather be going in an ambulance with all the lights flashing."

"Of course not. I'm glad it's turned out like this. But last time — well, we had a good laugh about it after. Remember, I woke you and you phoned my mother and asked her what time it was, and told me to sit still while you went to crash the car? Then when I laughed you thought I was hysterical. You looked so miserable I forgot what was going on trying to cheer you up."

She smiled.

"I expect you prefer it all organised, like this."

He didn't reply, but changed the subject.

"What about a name? We haven't got one yet."

"I'll know what to call her when I see her."

"How come you're so sure it's a girl? They wouldn't risk amnio-centesis, would they?"

"I told you, no. I just know it is, that's all."

"Sure you're sure?"

"Sure I'm sure," she answered without savour.

He wished she would liven up a bit.

"You're daft," he said, "you just want a girl so you can have the set."

She didn't rise to that.

"No, it's a girl. I can't even look forward to finding that out."

She looked down a tree-lined road to the sea. With something like boredom she recognised an ungainly figure in a white raincoat pushing a high, old-fashioned pram along the promenade.

"Shall we take the back road," asked James. "There's plenty of time. It's not even nine o'clock."

"Alright," she said, and he turned the car up the hill. Trees, gardens, moorland – all slipped past her indifferent gaze.

"It's time, it's time," she kept thinking, " – time to what? Time to die. 'That time of year thou mightest in me behold...' is that how it goes? 'Now it is autumn and things begin to die and rot...' Oh, I must stop thinking like this. What a waste."

Aloud, she said,

"What a waste this summer's been."

"It can't be a waste if you're alright," he said firmly. He had said it before.

"Oh, yes, you're right, of course," she answered, but felt doubt gathering like rain clouds. "I just feel something's come to an end but I don't know what."

At the hospital she was admitted briskly and wheeled off to her room. The brief flurry of action cheered her a little but it didn't last. Once she was in bed and James stood beside her shifting from foot to foot everything stopped again. She felt a burst of impatience at him. He looked as if he had accidentally bitten off a piece of lemon and couldn't think how to get rid of it.

"Why don't you sit and visit properly?" she snapped.

"Just for a minute then," he sat and tugged at his moustache. "I have to get back for Robbie."

"He'll be alright with Tracy."

"She's awful young."

"She's old enough to have a baby of her own."

"Oh, I know that — but Robbie's had a rough time this summer, with you not being able to see to him. I think he's had enough of strangers."

"Ach, I've been about the house all the time. I talked to him — read him stories."

"Aye, I suppose so. It's not the same, though."

"Havers. You just want to get back and bask in Tracy's crush."

She remembered the afternoon when Tracy had come round to offer her services, unasked. She had lolled in the doorway in a tight pink tee-shirt, her breasts soft and neat and conical — just waiting to be handled. James had had a good look.

"I know you," she said.

"I suppose so," he answered, smiling wryly.

"Don't get too big-headed. She's got most of the men in the neighbourhood in her sights. You're no exception. I wish I'd had her confidence at that age."

"Okay, okay. I'm a dumplin'," he said irritably.

"No, you're not. You're a hunk — that's why I keep such a close eye on you."

"Is that what you do?" he said and gazed past her out of the window.

She grappled with her feelings. It was true — she was jealous. She had discovered there were women younger and prettier than herself. It was unfair that because she was female the passage of time would leave her beached, but James would continue to be attractive and — worse — potent. She was very uncomfortable with the thought.

"I'd better get back, all the same," he said, "I'll be back at three with Robin."

"Alright," it was time to let go, "I'll see you later, then."
He kissed her swiftly, and left her to feel anxious.

"It's been so long since I let him make love to me," she thought, "I hope he doesn't get...notiony."

She didn't detail what she meant by 'notiony'. It could cover anything from indolent sensuality to raging lust. Not that she had ever noted either of these in James. He went about sex at a smooth, regular pace. But she's heard that men deprived of their usual sexual release got...notiony. Sternly she opened a magazine.

"I'm getting silly," she told the young thing prancing in tight, pale jeans to sell sanitary towels. "After all it was me brought the subject up. I'm his wife," she said to a woman caressing a bottle of bleach, "and very attractive — everyone says so."

She immersed herself in a story about a young woman who was trapped in a highly charged liaison with a heartless and over-sexed brute. She couldn't see the point of it. After a very early lunch nurses set about her body. Two of them came in wearing caps and masks. One of them was pushing a trolley with gloves and sheets of paper, a kidney bowl, a big roll of paper, green plastic razors and a big bottle of pink liquid.

"Oh, no!" she said.

"We're here to give you a wee shave," said the nurse brightly.

"I thought you didn't bother any more."

"Not usually — but things might get tricky with you so..."

"Rats!" said Hester and pressed her thighs together.

The nurses took no notice. In that snappy way they have they folded the sheet down and took up their places on either side of her.

"Could you bend your legs up, please?" said one. She wasn't expecting a refusal and she didn't get one. They slid a long piece of paper under her, put on plastic gloves and squirted cold shaving cream in the direction of her arse. She stared at the ceiling while they scraped away. It felt rough, like a cat licking her. The nurses were going on about a sister who had it in for one of them — or so they thought. Hes realised the one with the razor had just brought the other in so they could have a rap over her ventilated bum. She felt feverish. She told me,

"Last time this happened it was in the middle of labour. One nurse was taking my blood pressure, one was timing my contractions and everyone else was running about daft. This is so cold-blooded I'm like a fish on a slab."

Her fanny was naked, cold and forlorn.

"There you are," chirped the nurse, "— no problem."

"Until it starts to grow again," grumbled Hes. She wasn't going to give an inch. "It's horrible, then."

"Not for long."

"Long enough," she said as they flicked the paper away and pulled the sheet up.

"D'you want a fresh towel," asked the nurse.

She shook her head.

"Doctor'll be in in a minute."

On the strength of a whole six month's experience they decided she was going to be difficult. Threatened miscarriages were often difficult, they said.

Mr Stewart strolled in and smiled at Hes, who smiled back.

"All ready for tomorrow, now?" he asked.

"I suppose so," she answered.

He took it that this tepid response was a result of anxiety. She wasn't anxious, she was tepid. He could *have found this out if he had bothered to ask. Nothing was very pleasant, but then it wasn't very unpleasant, either. He started to put her in the picture, as he had done three times already.*

"Tomorrow morning I'll take you into theatre and give you an anaesthetic injection in the spine. Once that's working I'll give you an internal to see where the placenta is lying. If it's not too far down I'll strip your membranes and let labour take its course. If it is too far down — and let me say now that from what I've seen on the ultra sonic, I don't think it is, but it's better to be safe than sorry and have you bleeding catastrophically — if the placenta is too far down we'll give you a Caesarian. All clear?"

She nodded.

"You won't feel a thing, so you've nothing to worry about."

"Hah!" she thought, then she said,

"Why didn't you examine me sooner to find out where the placenta is lying?"

"Ah, well. If it's very low it wouldn't like being handled. All sorts of nasty things could have happened."

He gave her his best dimples.

"Like what?" she grated. She had to be sure her useless summer had been worthwhile. If he'd tried to leave without giving her that she was ready to grab him by the throat.

"Well..." he was wondering how much of this she could take on board. Doctors always assume laymen are morons. It makes them feel smart. What would be really smart would be to explain things better, but they don't seem to think of that.

"The placenta would have gone mad. It would have started producing all sorts of antibodies. You would have developed a fever — the baby's nourishment would have been interfered with..."

"I see."

"All right." It was an instruction.

"Yes."

"I'll see you tomorrow, then."

"Not if I see you first."

"Eh? Oh, I see. Ha ha. That's more like it. Cheerio, then."

He cleared out, his white coat flapping, and told the nurses her morale was good. That was his way of saying she had eased his worries.

She had a small rage banked up under her ribs.

"You'd better get it right," she thought, and kept on thinking it until the night when a couple of nembies took her out.

The next morning, before she could even see, she was given an enema, painted pink and put into a paper shirt. She snatched the paper hat from the nurse and stuffed her hair into it, then stuffed her legs into the leggings.

"If I must look a freak, let me at least do it to myself," she raged at them. Anger rode on the trolley with her to the operating theatre, where they groped about inside her, and when the doctor told her she would be going through labour she could have decked him.

"I thought I would be having a Caesarian," she complained. She knew she wasn't, but she liked winding him up.

"No, no," he said quickly, "You should be glad we won't have to. It would have left your womb dangerously weak."

He was paddling in her amnion in his neat green wellies.

"So?"

"Well, it would give you a problem when you have more children. You could only have two more."

"I'm not going to have any more children," she shouted, "Not two, not even one."

He exchanged glances with the midwife like parents over a kid in a pet.

"Even so, it's major surgery, and should be avoided if possible."

"We only operate as a last resort," the midwife supplied.

"You don't operate," snapped Hes. "The surgeons operate."

The midwife ignored her.

Hes rolled onto her side, folded her arms under her head and stared at the wall.

"We'll take you to the Birth Suite," said the midwife and hauled on the trolley.

"Birth Suite!" said Hes. "How bloody naff can you get?"

The midwife ignored her.

In the delivery room she flopped from the trolley to the bed like a seal over rocks. The midwife told her to hold her tummy and time her contractions. Then she said,

"Just a wee jag, now," and jammed a hose-pipe into her arm.

Hes looked down and saw that it was really a hypodermic needle which the nurse linked up to a bag of clear fluid. The fluid was cold and chilled her arm.

"Couldn't you have warmed it up a bit?" she asked.

"No, sorry," said the midwife, only she wasn't sorry at all. "We're very busy so I'll have to leave you for a minute. Don't run away, now."

Leaving them on their own was her way of punishing bad patients. Hes looked around. On her left there was a window and beside that a table with scales, a heap of green folded cloth and a lot of clear plastic tubes.

"What're they waiting for?" she asked, and her

stomach got hard. She rapped it with her knuckles but felt nothing.

"I should time it," she said and we looked round for a clock. There was one on the wall with a second sweep that wobbled as it moved.

"Where's my bloody watch?"

"In your bloody locker," I told her.

"Forget it," she said, and lay back.

Someone brought her a magazine but there was no time to read it, the contractions came so fast. A nurse came in and put a notice in red letters at the foot of her bed. It said, 'NO FOOD'.

"Why?!" said Hes.

"Oh, well, you might have to go back to theatre."

"Then why not tell me that and I can see I don't eat."

"Pardon?"

"Never mind."

A midwife came in in theatre mask, paper hat and green smock. At least we thought she was a midwife, because she asked her to roll over and pull her knees up. For all we knew it might have been someone who was queer for pregnant women. After this had happened a few times five people came in wearing green gowns and paper hats and masks.

"Where's the party?" asked Hes.

"Pardon?"

"Oh, never mind."

They pulled the sheet off the bed and draped her in green cloth from the waist down. They clipped her feet into metal webbing. They peered up her fanny.

"Could you give us a push, please," they asked. She took in a big breath and pushed.

"Lovely," they said.

This went on for a while then there was a wail from

the middle of the gang at her rump. So far as we could
tell the baby had arrived.

"You were right," said James. "It is a girl. How are you feeling?"

"I don't know. Sore, now, of course, but it was all such a non-event. I remember when Robbie was born..."

Hearing his name, Robin looked up from the floor where he was battering a present for the baby. Hes stopped because she didn't think childbirth was a suitable topic for his ears.

The nurse brought in the clear plastic crib containing a tiny, peeled human. James looked at his daughter solemnly.

"What're we going to call her, then?"

"Nerine."

"Say again."

"Nerine — three syllables — she was a sea nymph — the daughter of Nereus."

"That's a bit heavy, isn't it?"

"She'll cope. I've managed to live with Hesione all these years."

"Nerine Grieve. I suppose it sounds okay."

"You don't have to take it, of course. I just fancy it."

"No — it's only fair. I chose Robin for him."

He picked the boy up, held him over the crib and told him to say hello to his sister. Hes recalled his birth again — the speed, the light, the intensity and the exhilaration. James in tears wiping the sweat from her face and blowing his nose on the same hanky. The staff full of praise so that she felt like a little girl in her first party dress. And at the climax, when they told her to hold back, the urgency — "I don't care if I split — I don't care if I split the whole length of my spine — I must push NOW!!"

A nurse bounced in and smiled at James.

"Well, what do you think of your new daughter, then?"

"She's beautiful," he said, lying. "She looks...fit."

"She's doing very well. They're both doing well," she beamed at them all and her eye fell on Robbie.

"Is that you got the full set, now?"

He nodded and glanced at Hester. The nurse went on blithely,

"We'll be moving them to the main ward tomorrow, so don't come looking for them here."

Hesione watched a silverfish quivering on the wall beside her wooden locker.

"That will be nice," she said carefully.

9

Sea king's daughter from over the sea...

Hesione was at odds with the nurses. For one thing she
was having trouble sleeping. In the five nights since the
baby was born she had not been able to sleep for more
than two hours together, and that only lightly. After the
babies had been taken to the nursery she lay on the hard
hospital bed reading until the nurses thought she had
done enough. Then they would come over and whisper
their objections and she would put her book away and
begin her night watch.

For the first three nights she had made the usual effort
to sleep — lying on one side, then the other — rearrang-
ing her pillows — taking cups of tea and sleeping pills
from the nurses and going to the bathroom for the change
of scene. But now she lay still. She was afraid she had
worn out the nurse's sympathy and the next stage would
only be stronger and stronger sleeping pills. From life
with her mother she had found that people dedicated to
helping others get frightened when their help is of no
use. Nurses were there to make sure the new mothers

got a rest, and if she did not rest she would be classified as a "bad" patient and coerced accordingly.

If asked for the reason for this restlessness she would have named two factors. One was the lochia oozing out of her which seemed too plentiful, too thick and too dark. It had not been like this the last time, she was sure, but the staff told her it was nothing to worry about. But this year she had spent too long with her thighs chafed by towels and her thoughts on the wetness of her vulva. She wanted it to be over. She wanted to be clean.

During puberty the thick, clear mucous she discharged had upset her. She had been on holiday that summer in Greece with friends of the family. There she had learned the joy of swimming in clear, warm water. Each day she had swum out to the rocks in the bay and stayed there, the lower half of her body submerged, feeling the joy of an endless supply of clean salt water scouring off her secretions. She would love to do that now. Every time she moved in the bed her towel slid around dangerously.

And her daughter was going down the same weary road. On her fourth morning Hesione had unwrapped the nappy from the tiny red thighs and found it damp and smeared with red. She had to hang onto the sides of the crib. Everything on the rim of her vision faded and she found she was staring down a long tunnel at her baby who waved her limbs gently like seaweed; who stretched her hands like tentacles; who smiled lazily to herself.

All at once she was on the floor with a nurse kneeling beside her. She was carted off to bed and an auxilliary finished cleaning the baby.

The other reason for the lack of sleep was the tenderness of her breasts. She could not bring herself to breast-feed, and the pills they had given her to "scatter" her milk had not been effective. This was another source of aggravation to the nurses.

Yes, she knew the lore — "breast is best". Everyone had told her that, including her mother, since she was four months gone with Robbie. Yes, she knew it was better for both mother and baby — it tones up the womb and gives the baby antibodies. She knew it, but she couldn't face it. She couldn't expose a private part of herself to a total stranger. That's how she felt, and no amount of nagging was going to change it. Her only ally in the family was James's mother. She told her son that breast-feeding was unsafe and unsound.

"If you give them a bottle, you know what they're getting. And a nice glass bottle — you can see when it's clean. You cannae with...the other."

James stayed neutral.

When the staff brought her the bottle at feeding time they handed it too her with such mincing expressions of disgust that she would not have been surprised to see them handling it with tongs. All around her the other mothers were clucking and bearing their bosoms to their babies. She was surrounded by strange growths of pink, white and blue fungus which erupted, dripping, at four-hourly intervals. Miserable, she shrank with her face averted from this exhibition, and fed her deprived infant from a hard, sterile glass bottle. Yet in spite of her wishes the front of her nightie would get wet and at night she couldn't rest because her swollen breasts made it impossible to lie in comfort.

By now the nights had fallen into a routine she almost enjoyed. To start with she would lie on her side with an open book and listen to the other three mothers settling down. Two went off to the lounge for a last cigarette. She would hear them coming back — swishing along the corridor in their slippers, their voices quiet. Their locker doors would clack as they took out their sponge-bags; they would swish off again to the bathroom and back. If her light was on they would call good-night and she would answer brightly so that they wouldn't think her a snob. Then the creak and rustle as they got into bed, the muttered conversation, exchange of biscuits and the final rebuke from the nurse, and silence would fall.

Hesione's night had begun.

Lying in the dark she could retune her senses. She would listen for the nurses and auxilliaries in the corridor, whisking past in their tight nylon dresses. Beyond that, in the kitchen, she could listen for talk and laughter and the clang of the kettle. If she really stretched her ears, she could hear, farthest of all, the babies piping and yammering in the nursery. Beside her the mothers were heaps of bedding and smudges on the pillow. If the nurses were away she would sit up and then she might catch one of them lying supine with her head thrown back and her mouth open. This would upset her, but she had found that if she switched on the light over her bed the offender would roll over to get the glare out of her eyes, and Hes could relax again.

Finally she got into the habit of watching her companions for when they turned into these supine horrors. She would sniff the air for the smell of rotting blubber, and listen for the sound of their breathing. She told herself not to be silly and turned her attention to the comings and goings of the staff like a child listening to the murmur of the family around them in the night.

Sometimes she worried about changing, herself.

On the fifth night, at about three in the morning, she fell asleep and felt the world slipping out from under her.

She landed on her feet with a jolt that snapped her awake. Her heart was thudding as she worked out her situation. It was dark. Somehow she was wearing her dressing-gown — she could feel it under her hand. On her feet she had her thin leather slippers and through them she could feel that the ground was uneven, possibly rocky. A sea-smelling breeze blew past her face. She waited for her eyes to adjust to the dark.

The time passed slowly, but at last she began to pick things out. As her sense of smell had suggested, she was near the sea, standing on a low cliff above a beach. She could not yet see the water, but she could hear the suck and draw of the waves on shingle. In the far distance a line of grey told her that dawn was not far off.

On her right the land rose high and black. She drew in a deep, unsteady breath. The air was mild and clear. Questions hunted across her mind — "shall I wait here? — it's too dark to move safely — how high am I? — where is this place? — is it far to the hospital? — where's the road? — how long till day? — how long till they miss me?"

She stooped to find a place to sit. Her hand ran over dew-soaked thrift and some rocks, all too wet to sit on. As she straightened again something flew out of the darkness. It tangled, squeaking, in her hair and flew off. She was startled, but told herself it must be nothing more than a bat on its way home. When she bent down again to find a dry place to sit more bats dived at her and she raised her hands to fend them off. She could hear the flap of their leather wings and see the glint of eyes in the growing light. They seemed to be coming from the seaward side. All at once she realised that she was being driven — herded inland, toward, or away, from something.

"Perhaps they live in a cave on the beach and they're mobbing me to get me away."

She felt behind her with a foot and took a cautious step. They became more frantic in their attack and dived at her, striking her in the face and chest. She turned away and wrapped her arms round her head to protect it. Several of them hit her back at once. In a panic, now, she began to walk across what she hoped was machair. The action of the creatures made no sense; they might do anything and she was alone and lost. She increased her pace. Fifty paces on she fell screaming into a crevice in the rock.

The crack, as it turned out, was wide, and the side she had fallen against was sloping and sandy so that she slithered down gently to land on a mat of seaweed. It was wet and slimy and she scrambled off it in haste and shook herself. She seemed to have come to no harm apart from some smarting where she had grazed her ankle.

"I've been very lucky," she said aloud, to convince herself. Her voice shook, however, and she was trembling all over. She took time to steady herself. Fresh air wafted past her up the crevice.

"If I follow that air current I should find a way out of here," she said in a more controlled voice. There was no echo.

"It's a good job I'm not given to claustrophobia — this must be a very small space."

She raised her arms and began to feel her way along the walls of the tunnel towards the source of the air current. It was difficult to keep track of time and it seemed hours before, with a sob of joy, she saw a blob of light ahead. The light was dim and turned out to be nothing more than light from yet another tunnel. When she came to the bend she saw with dismay that the light was pale, green and came, not from reflected daylight, but from the walls themselves. They were coated with a natural luminous substance.

She heard voices coming from around the curve ahead and retreated back to her bend to await developments.

With growing horror she listened as the sound of the voices was joined by the sound of something else. They were all moving very slowly toward her and she waited in agony for their arrival. She did not dare to look out in case they should see her, and as she listened she realised that she did not want to see them.

The voices were loud and vicious. They were accompanied by the cracking of a whip, and with them came a bubbling moan and a regular swish and scrape. Drifting toward her came the familiar stench of blood and oil and rotting fish. She pressed herself against the wall of her tunnel and prayed that she would be passed by.

At last she thought she heard the sounds retreating and inched her head out scarcely breathing. She was seized by the arm and dragged into the middle of the main tunnel.

"We've been expecting you," said a hoarse voice.

She looked down into a pair of cloudy brown eyes. They belonged to a little man who had his hair combed sleek against his head, a receding chin and four-fingered, thumbless hands. He was wearing a dark brown tunic and leggings, and she looked at the others and saw that they were all very similar. It was the menfolk of the seal-women.

Raising her eyes reluctantly she tried to see what it was they had been driving down the tunnel. To her relief it was too far along for her to see clearly. All she could make out was a black, hulking shape which seemed to be hauling itself along on flippers. The bubbling moans of anguish it uttered were at once pitiful and disgusting. She looked at the floor and saw that the monster had left a trail of dark slime.

"What are you doing to that poor creature," she demanded.

"He is our ruler," replied the small man in a thick, phlegmy voice.

"But you're treating him like a slave."

"He is our ruler," he repeated then sank his claws into her arm. "Come with me," he said and dragged her, stumbling, after him.

She braced her feet against the rocky floor and brought him to a halt.

"What is it you want from me this time?" she gasped.

"You still owe us — you'll have to pay."

"What do I owe you? You've done nothing for me. I've never seen you before."

"You took a life — you saved a life. You are still in our debt."

"What can I owe you?"

"Service," he croaked.

"But I could do nothing for that woman."

"That makes no difference. Whether you meant to or not, you still brought about her death."

"But that makes no sense. I was taken to help her against my will. I knew nothing about her. Her death was an unfortunate accident. It may have been my hands on her when she died, but her death was an accident. I was forced to be there."

"That makes no difference. Your are responsible and you must pay us what is due."

Hesione felt panic rising. In her world this argument would be nonsense, but here it seemed completely reasonable. This was terrifying. The man and she had no common ground and she was the one who was alone and helpless.

"How can it be that I owe you something? I saved the baby's life, you agree. That should redress the balance. I can't do more than that.

"Her mother is dead. You will not care for her. She will not survive. You must pay."

"But I'm only human. What could I do for a seal

child?"

"You are a human, that means you know more than us. You are our ruler; you made us. You must help now."

"If I know more than you how is it I let you catch me out?"

"You made us, and you let us through."

This made no more sense than the rest of his speech. Suddenly he tugged at her arm and she skidded in the slime on the floor.

"I don't want you," she shrieked. "I don't want to be here. If I'm your ruler as you say, you must obey me. I command you to let me go from here!"

He laughed and shouted to the others,

"She does not want to be here!"

The others laughed, and their laughter filled the tunnel. The monster's moans grew louder. One of them cracked a whip.

"I don't want to be like that thing," she thought, but the little man read her mind.

"You had better go," he said, suddenly, and pushed her furiously against the wall. She hit her head on the rock and started to sink into it. It came to her then that if she passed through the wall she would be in the tunnel under her own house.

"No!" she yelled, "I don't want to be there!"

James would be terrified to find her at home. He would be soiled by this knowledge, as she was.

"I can't go there."

As when she had fainted before, the world disappeared in a slow blink, leaving her at last with a narrow picture of a sly, brown face. She came to consciousness lying on her bed in hospital. A nurse was shaking her and telling her it was five-thirty. She groped her way to the shower and there found her ankle was grazed and her slippers stained.

"Have I been sleep-walking?" she asked the night nurse.

"No."

The nurse took her to the door of her room and pointed down the corridor to the nurse's station.

"There's someone there all night," she explained, "and no-one could get past her without being seen. We would have seen you. Okay?"

She sent Hes to get her baby from the nursery. On her way back the nurse stopped her again. She was carrying a thick note-book.

"This is our log of the night's happenings. You're down as having got up to the toilet at two thirty-five and going back. That's all."

"Thanks," said Hes. "It was just that I walked in my sleep once when I was pregnant and I thought I might have done it again."

She showed her the graze on her ankle.

"Ach, would you look at that," said the nurse, annoyed. "I'm always telling them the mosaic tiles in the shower are too rough. There's been a few like that. You don't feel the bang when you're showering, 'cause you're wet, then you find the blood when you're getting dried. Has it stopped bleeding? I can get you a plaster."

"No, it's fine. That'll be where it happened — the shower. It's nothing to worry about."

Showering also explained the water stains on her new slippers. But it didn't explain the grains of sand trapped between the sole and the upper. She showed them to James at visiting time. His explanation was that she had picked up the sand one time when she had worn them in the garden. After that she left the matter lie, because she didn't want to hear him realise that she had not worn the slippers till she came to the hospital and begin to wonder how the sand had got there. Under no circumstances could she have talked about her vile "dreams", because just to think about them made her brain crawl. If she went so far as to talk about them her brain would melt and shrivel like a salted slug.

James was visiting on his own that night. Charlotte had volunteered to help out for a few days as term was not yet started. Hes was pleased to think she was there. It would keep Tracy at bay and James was in no danger from her sister. He had confessed to Hes that her waspish manner had scared him even when he was going out with her.

They hung over the crib looking at the baby. The clear plastic box reminded them both of a fish tank. The baby was wrapped in a blanket. Her skin was cleared, and so fine that the creases showed blue. Her head was covered with white fuzz and her tiny folded fist lay in front of her face, pink and crumpled. Her mouth twitched as she dreamed of feeding.

"There was a time when I was like that." thought Hesione, "Once I was sealed and perfect. Gravity hadn't dragged at my flesh to make it sag and hang — children hadn't stretched my skin beyond its capacity to shrink back to shape — my tissues were intact. But everything has been forced out of place. My stomach is covered with shiny white lines. Once my vagina was like hers, small — almost invisible — my vulva was pale and chubby. Now my vagina is a passage for others to use at will and my vulva is brown and flabby..."

She cut this line of thought of violently — shocked to her roots that she could think like this. Never since adolescence had she thought so much about her privy parts, and even then not in such downright terms.

The baby smiled knowingly and opened her eyes for a moment.

"She's windy," said James, the experienced father. "D'you think I should burp her?"

"She'll be alright. Bottle-fed babies are less colicky than...the others."

"Oh." He was put out. "When will you be getting home?"

"It's usually eight days — no — the seventh day after the baby is born — for the first one and the fifth for all the others. But that's in normal cases. In my case I'm not sure. The nurses won't give anything away and refer me to the doctor. I think they're hinting it won't be Saturday — in my case."

In fact the nurses had hinted at nothing. In fact she wanted to be kept in longer. It was not that she didn't want to go home, but that she was enjoying her status as 'The Threatened Miscarriage' and if she were sent home at the same time as the other mothers she would just be another healthy young mum.

"I'll see if I can find a doctor and get some sense out of him. Dr. Stewart won't be here this late, will he?"

"Mr Stewart," she corrected him absently.

"Mr Stewart, then."

"I don't know. He could be. I've seen him later than this if he wants to speak to one of the husbands or something."

"There's sure to be a registrar at least."

"Sure to be," she said, wondering when he would turn and see the doorway forming in the wall beside him.

Silence fell. He tried to revive the conversation.

"I went to the registry office today."

"Good. Did they have any trouble with the name?"

"They didn't bat an eyelid. The woman even offered to put a couple of dots over the 'e'. I told her not to bother."

"Fine."

That exhausted the subject.

"So..." he battled on, "she's not reading yet?"

"No. Not yet. We'll have to give her a week or two."

"I can see you've been neglecting her. What will your mother say?"

"Oh, yes. She's definitely deprived," she murmured.

She was watching the wall carefully. The opening was wider, and reached all the way to the floor. She knew she could stop it if he would leave her alone, but as long as she had to go on making conversation she couldn't remember what she had to do.

"She's doing alright, then," he persisted.

"Just fine," she replied and started to slide down the bed. If she lay down he would think she was tired and leave her alone. She knew this because it had worked before, at home. For a while longer he tried to get her to talk, and she continued to slide down until she was flat on her back. He was non-plussed.

"Well," he said, putting his hands on his thighs and levering himself up, "There's still a lot to do in the house, and you're tired..."

"Yes," she agreed wanly, "I am rather tired today."

Then what he had said sank in. She sat up.

"What do you have to do at home?"

"I've all the washing to do tonight."

"Why tonight? What are you doing during the day?"

"Nothing. I just thought it would be better to do all the housework in the evening. It gives me more time with Robin during the day."

"That's cute."

"It's what I did last time you were in hospital." he said defensively, "You should try it."

"I will — I will."

She remembered then that he was telling the truth. Being a man he had not realised that housework was a daytime job. She also remembered her argument at the time and revived it.

"Only will you please tell me what will happen to our social life?"

"I don't mean all the time. Just some evenings. The washing machine's cheaper at night."

She cut him off.

"That reminds me — you'd best take that book back to Karen."

Leaning over at a perilous angle she reached into her locker.

"I'll get it," he began, but she whipped up again and handed him a book.

"But I only brought it yesterday."

"I don't want it. It's got a funny stain on it — on page eighteen, look!"

He looked and found a reddish-brown finger print at the foot of the page.

"She's drinking too much," muttered Hes, "— she's turning into a slut."

"Don't be daft — one wee stain? That doesn't mean a thing. What's the matter with you?"

His irritation was clear to her and she backed down at once.

"I suppose it doesn't. I'm sorry. I'm feeling a bit edgy tonight. You'll have to forgive me."

To her surprise she saw that the doorway was closing up again. All the same she hoped he would go because she had to think about it and she was relieved when he said,

"Well I think I'll go and get hold of the doctor now, before visiting time ends and all the other dads join the queue."

"Cheerio, then," she said at once, and watched him threading his way out between the other visitors.

1 0
Renounce the devil and all his ways.

Hesione watched autumn spreading. The trees were swindled out of sap so that the leaves changed colour, then the wind wrenched the leaves from the trees to the ground where a white fur of frost grew along their veins. By day the sun was warm enough to melt the frost, but in the night the grip that cold had on the landscape grew steadily stronger. On the moors above the town the bracken curled, turned from green to red to brown and died; grass faded from emerald to topaz and heather bled down from purple to bronze. She thought it cruel that this spectacle of colour could only be produced by plants dying.

In the sea the seals were heading for the mating grounds. Their progress was unhurried, and Hesione was sure that for some days she had seen the same one in the bay at the foot of the hill. There were many days to go before the assembly at the haul-outs would be complete and some of the immature ones liked to take a last holiday before beginning the serious business of reproduction.

Males of all generations and females — with young and without — would all be returning to the place where they were conceived.

After the upheaval of the return from hospital, life had settled quickly into a soothing routine. Then all at once James had disrupted this when he announced that he wanted to see more of his children. He asked, no demanded, that they should stay up later at night so that he could play with them when he got home from work. Hester was horrified.

"We can't do that! Babies have to be in bed by seven at the latest. We can't keep them up till all hours."

"Why not? As long as they get their quota of sleep what does it matter when it starts?"

"But it'll make our evenings much shorter. We won't have time to sit before we have to go to bed."

"We can go to bed a bit later. Anyway, why should we just sit. It's boring. Look, I took the job on that antiquated industrial estate, at that geriatric firm because we wanted to live in the country but I didn't want to spend three hours a day commuting. If I don't get to see my kids I've wasted myself for nothing."

He had had time to muster his arguments and she needed notice to assemble her defence. She rallied weakly.

"But what about the mornings?"

"What about them? If they sleep longer so can you. You're looking tired these days."

"I hate sleeping in. I have to get up and get on with my work."

If she had hoped to make him feel guilty she was unlucky.

"That's a great idea. You could finish off your work quickly and then give them your undivided attention."

She capitulated.

One afternoon her mother, the power behind James's assault, arrived without warning. She explained that her class were off to a show and she had a free afternoon so she decided to drop in. Twenty-seven miles is a helluva long drop so we knew she was up to something.

"This is what she does when she's got something to say that she can't bring up in front of the old man." I said.

"Shut up," said Hes. *"I know. Just let her get round to it. I'm not going to give her an inch."*

After tea and a long time spent manoevering for an opening, Helen got to the point.

"I was over at Bearsden the other day to see Auntie Ellen. You know, that house is far too big for her to manage. She should just sell up and move in with Laura. I know they don't get on terribly well but they could easily split that big place up into two flats."

We kept quiet and watched her. She had to get on with it.

"Well, anyway, Ellen was wondering when the christening is going to be because she's wanting to go down and visit Amy."

Helen always talks about the family when she needs reassurance. It's her version of rosary beads — click, Laura, click, Amy, click, Ellen, and click — the biggest bead of all — auntie Maidie who is loaded and everybody is nice to her because she might disinherit them only they don't put it like that because it would be vulgar. Hesione tried a stall.

"We weren't planning a christening for Neri."

Helen hadn't even heard her. She went on,

"I was thinking it should be here this time. Now that Mr Daly's gone there's no point in getting Ellen and the other old dears to come all the way over to the South Side. Anyway the new man wouldn't suit them

at all. He has people playing guitars in front of the Communion Table and that sort of thing. What's your minister like?"

"I haven't the faintest idea. As I have told you we never go to church. This is why I don't feel right going just to get the children baptised. They're not likely to become communicants."

"That's what you said about Robin's christening."

"At least I'm consistent," mumbled Hes.

"And my answer is the same, too. It's for the old ones. They like to see the kiddies right."

"But it doesn't mean anything. It's only mumbo-jumbo."

"If it doesn' mean anything why should you object to it happening."

"That was your argument to my father. You told me that last time, too."

"That's right. And he had to admit that he couldn't, in conscience, object."

"Yes, but it's a lot of trouble to go to if you don't believe in it."

"Oh, I wouldn't expect you to do anything about it. It's my notion and even if we don't do it at home — I mean at my house — I'll see to the catering and everything. That's only fair."

"I couldn't let you do that."

"Of course you can, dear. You should be used to it by now. I ran things here for most of the summer."

"I get it," thought Hes, "now I have to cough up for services rendered. Well, I can still try for a postponement. Neri's not even a month old."

Her mother could handle that, too. The minister would need notice anyway. They should see him as soon as possible, however, because the man might be busy.

We could still hope that he would refuse to service a bunch of heathens. Hes was reluctant to broach the matter with James until she was definitely lumbered, but she was crossed again, for the next thing we knew, Helen had spoken to the guy and he had bidden us to an audience on the Tuesday evening. Hes explained to James why he had to baby-sit and apologised for the coming invasion but he just shrugged. As long as his folks didn't get dropped off the invitation list he was content to go along with it.

Already we could see the aunts, ducking their heads under feather hats and failing to resist the temptation to peer at Hes's gear. There would be Auntie Maidie, with her skin brown and wrinked like lime-bark and with her her faithful toady, Alice — shoulders curved and belly jutting as if someone had pulled her spine out and let her collapse like melting blancmange — she helped give this impression herself by always wearing blancmange coloured clothes. The full glare of a family gathering was a version of hell with clicking dentures, concrete perms, gold-framed specs and a lot of ugly people — and I'm not talking about their bodies.

Off we went to the manse. The minister was was waiting for us in a book-lined study that had been designed a century before to put the frighteners on the lower ranks. It might have succeeded, too, if it hadn't been clear from the dust on the shelves that the books hadn't been handled for about ninety-nine years. The desk he sat behind was a modest little thing barely wider than a tennis court and covered with green leather that looked like it had been put on before the cow was dead.

He stood when Hes and Helen walked in and held out his hand for the handshake but when they couldn't reach him across the his desk he used the hand to point to a couple of chairs. It turned out he wasn't bothered about the fact that Hes and James weren't church people — let's face it, everyone's got to hustle these days. When she told him, blushing crimson, that it was just to mollify the old ones he handed her a square, patronising smile.

"Now, Hesione," he began.

Hes was furious he had used her name.

"...I am a minister of the church, is that not so?"

She realised, late, that she was supposed to reply. Her timing shot to hell she answered lamely — 'Yes.'

"And as such I am supposed to be a good Christian..."

This time she nodded on cue. She was beginning to get the hang of it.

"...which means that I think the sacraments of the Church are important — not just for myself — for every human soul."

He was leaning across the desk so far his chin nearly hit the ink-well. Helen was nodding and smiling eagerly.

"That's just what I was telling her," she said.

He gave her a sour look — he was winding up for his climax and she was breaking up his rhythm.

"So..." The pause was too long. "it would be very wrong of me — indeed, I could never face myself again — if I were to refuse the right of baptism to anyone who asked for it!"

We stifled a desire to clap and cheer. Hes said,

"I see. Thank you," and clenched her teeth on a grin.

Helen rose and crossed over to the minister. For a nasty moment we thought she was going to kiss him. Instead she pulled out her diary and they started banging on about dates.

We sat back in the dusty armchair and watched. Whenever he stopped talking, we saw that his jaw clapped shut like a bread-bin. With his mane of white hair, carefully arranged to stick out all round like a sun-burst, he must have been one of the vainest people we had ever seen. Going on seventy and an ego like a two-year-old. His eyes were watchful, all the same, in case someone should step out of line and disagree with him. He was the only one allowed to tell people their place.

The only things that didn't fit the picture of a minister were his hands. They had fat red fingers more like a butcher than a man of the cloth. Hes shuddered at the thought of them holding her baby.

"And that jaw!" she said to me, "he could take off the top of her head like a boiled egg. I can't let them do this."

"If you're going to stop them you'd better get on it right now," I told her. "If you leave it any longer there'll be no road back.

"What am I supposed to do? Jump up and run out of the room?"

"You can do anything you damn well please. You could even brain the minister with his inkwell. She's your fucking baby, or had you forgotten that?"

"I can't do that. My ma would have a stroke."

"So what? She knew you weren't keen on the christening."

"I can't do that to her. She's dead keen on it."

"Suit yourself."

"I mean, what the hell? It won't harm Neri to have a bit of water dropped on her head."

"It won't do her any good either. Who's in charge here, anyway?"

Suddenly we had to shut up. Something had happened in the room and her mother and the minister were looking at her with smiles fading off their faces.

"I'm sorry," said Hes, "I'm afraid I was miles away. I didn't hear the last..."

Helen turned her face to the minister — probably signalling to him something about Hes's state of mind. She said,

"You must excuse her. She's had a difficult time of it."

"It's quite alright," he answered breezily, "I've had lassies in here to arrange christenings and they couldn't get a word out for tears. They call it post-natal depression."

"Now I know what's wrong," Hes said to me, "isn't he a wonder? I don't know how I've managed without him all these years."

"The minister was saying he hasn't got a spare day for a month," said Helen, shouting at her as if she was deaf. "But he can pencil us in for November the fifth."

"Great," she yelled back, "can't he manage October 31st, though?"

"No, I'm terribly sorry," he boomed, missing the point, "That's the day before the feast of All Souls. I'll be very busy."

"I'm sure he will," said Hes to me, then aloud she said, "Bonfire night will be fine. I hope you'll enjoy our firework display."

I could have hugged her.

Helen's face turned full frontal to us and remodelled itself into the sort of scowl you only see on Kabuki masks.

"Splendid, splendid," the minister boomed on, "I hope I can get to see them."

"You'll be more than welcome," said Hes archly.

Her mother looked murderous.

As we waded out through the gravel in the manse's driveway she rounded on Hes.

"Hester, I'm surprised at you, making a fool of him like that. You, of all people."

"I didn't make a fool of him," she replied.

"Nature got there first," I added.

"Or if I did," she went on, biting back a smile, "he didn't notice, so it comes to the same thing. It doesn't matter."

"It most certainly does — a firework display, indeed!"

"What's wrong with that?"

"And what happens when he comes along looking for this display and you aren't having one? He'll realise then he's been made a fool of."

"Who says we're not having a firework display?"

"You can't have fireworks at a baptism!!"

"Why not? Now I come to think of it it'll be great. I'll get James to start work on it whenever I get back home. All this nonsense about the christening is for the crumblies but I don't see why we can't have some fun as well. My daughter's naming day should be something special for everyone. Robbie will love it. Maybe even Charlotte will come."

Her mother sighed.

"Be that as it may, you had no intention of having fireworks when you mentioned it first. You were making a gull of that nice old man. And going into a dwam like that in your chair — I don't know what to make of you."

We waited for the next line, and it came right on cue.

"You're going to have to pull yourself together, girl."

"He's not a nice old man," said Hes, choking on a giggle. "He's loathsome. You only say he's nice because he's a 'man of the cloth'. Those fat red fingers."

She shuddered.

"Well," said her mother, wrapping things up, as she thought, "there's plenty of time. If you can find a minister more to your taste you can change to him. I won't say a word."

"For the last time," Hesione snapped, "No minister

is to my taste. He'll do as well or as badly as any other. Just don't go trying to fool me into liking him. Let's get the bloody thing over. This is all to gratify your dottled relatives — no more."

She turned away to hide the grin that was spreading over her face. It was the first time she had ever spoken to Helen like that and the effect was gorgeous. Her mother's jaw had gone slack. Her mouth had stayed shut, but there was no doubt about the muscles around it. They had sagged.

Hes marched over to her mother's car, not angry, just wound up. She had moved all at once into a higher gear and couldn't keep still. Helen trotted after her wrapped in a chilly silence that was supposed to intimidate her. I knew it wouldn't, not now, so I took off.

Back in the car Helen tried once more to have the last word.

"I do think you ought to have it soon, dear. You never know what might..."

"What might what?"

"Oh, you know. If anything were to...happen to Neri."

"She's not going to die, if that's what you mean. The days are gone when a babe had to be snatched from childbed to the font to make sure it didn't spend eternity in Limbo. Don't tell me it's got to you after all. Next thing you'll be scratching her upper lip to ward off the evil eye."

"Scratching her lip? I never heard of such a thing!"

"Haven't you? They you were lucky. You must be grateful you never needed that kind of reassurance."

"I've always been grateful, of course, dear."

Hesione rounded on her.

"If she were to die let's hope that the God, if there is one, is more merciful than the one in your minister's theology. That God is so vindictive he'd keep a poor little baby out of heaven just because her lousy parents didn't get her baptised. The only God I want to know about is one with a better temper than that."

Her eyes had begun to sting as they always did when she talked about religion. Helen looked at her shrewdly.

"As you say, dear," she said quietly. "You've come through a lot in the last months."

Hesione didn't hear her. She was fighting an urge to pound her thigh with her fist. Her excitement was tremendous, but she was confident she could control it. In fact she was so confident that she nearly told her mother about it. Confidence had filled her from the head to the feet and she was glowing with it. She looked out of the car and cast this radiance over the people in the street. When her mother dropped her off she stood for a while in the garden and felt herself lighting up the whole avenue. She was surprised when a couple walking past didn't seem to notice it. She went into the house to make sure that her family got some at least.

James was reading in front of the television with the sound turned off. She stood beside him and watched to see what the programme was before she spoke to him. She saw seals on the screen and her interest quickened. A mother seal was lying supine in deep snow, suckling her white furry baby. The picture was of great calm and Hester said,

"Oh, well, she's alright, then."

James looked up at that and she smiled at him. When she looked back at the screen she saw a big, dark-clad man in sea-boots approaching mother and baby. The pup broke off feeding and humped merrily over the snow to greet the man. The man had a club and he hit the baby on the head. Blood appeared on the snow under the baby.

Then the man kicked it in the head, pulled out a knife and skinned it without making sure it was dead.

Hesione's fingers were clutching the back of the chair. Her mouth was gummed shut on a scream as if in a nightmare. She kept thinking how she would be alright if she could get out a scream. It would relieve the pressure building up inside her, because something had to relieve the pressure...

James caught her as she fell and laid her on the rug.

She revived in time to see the mother seal with eyes streaming tears and beside her a heap of red pulp being picked at by a seagull. As the gull tugged at a rubbery red streamer the television screen seemed to fill the whole space in front of Hesione's head. Her mouth yawned wide as the screen but still no sound issued to drive the pictures out. Instead her mouth started to close round the pictures and although she snatched her head away from the ruined air they forced themselves in under her skull, wet and red, wet and red, she couldn't bite them off. She could not squeeze them out.

"Ehhh!" she hissed.

James was very frightened. He thought she was having a fit as she lay at his feet writhing and twisting her head from side to side.

"Hester!" he shouted, for once forgetting the children upstairs. Then "Hesione," he cried, hoping that the other name might penetrate through her seizure.

"HESIONE!"

Suddenly she lay still and opened her eyes. Her gaze was distant, but at least it was intelligent.

"I'm so sleepy," she said.

He took her up to bed and helped her to undress.

"I'm going to be sick," she announced and he rushed to get a bowl which she filled neatly. He took it away and came back to sit beside her.

"I've never been sick in front of you before," she remarked.

"What happened?"

"When?"

"Just now!"

"Ugly things," she muttered, frowning slightly. "I won't think about them."

"I'm going to get the doctor."

"If you like."

The doctor came quickly and shone lights into her eyes. He said,

"It's probably nothing to worry about, but keep an eye on her for a few days in case something like it happens again."

Hes knew it wouldn't happen again. She was going to see it did not.

The doctor injected her with a sedative and left.

1 1

The pleasant land of Counterpane

As soon as James had left room she sat up and listened until she was sure he had gone all the way downstairs. Then she lay down again and arranged herself in a cocoon of duvet. In an instant the images clamouring for attention in her mind spread out in a swathe all around her and swept her off the bed.

She landed on her side with a sickening jar and blacked out. When she opened her eyes it was too dim to see anything, but as her eyes adjusted she saw a faint red illumination which showed black shapes surrounding her. She felt that she was lying up to her waist in warm water and there were rocks underneath her, digging into her side. When she tried to lever herself up on one hand it sank to the wrist in something soft and slimy. Hastily she pulled her hand clear of the muck and bent over to rinse it in the water round her knees. The liquid was thick and sticky and it *was borne in on her that it was not water, but her mind recoiled at the thought of what it really was. Suddenly, as if someone had pulled a switch, she found smells registering on her senses. And began to retch.*

With streaming eyes she lay convulsing helplessly as wave after wave of nausea swept over her. Each breath she drew in filled her mouth and throat with a choking miasma composed of all the smells that had haunted her before with the addition of something she could not identify. The wrenching in her stomach left her weaker and weaker with each spasm, and it occurred to her that if it did not stop she would soon die. At last the retching subsided and she lay trembling and spent, able to hope at last that her stomach would not tear itself apart. Indifferent to the pool of vomit under her head she was grateful to lie still. She opened her mouth a little and allowed air to leak into her lungs. She gagged for a moment when the smell of vomit joined the others but that soon passed. Cautiously she inhaled through her nose and wondered at her own resilience.

She tried to sit up, but her muscles had nothing left. She sank back onto the slimy stones and fell into an unpleasant sleep. When she woke again it was dawn and the clouds were streaked with dull, angry reds like a discarded sanitary towel. At last she was able to sit up and study the landscape. The liquid she was lying in was, indeed, blood, thick and half-clotted. She was on a shingle of brown and ochre rocks overlaid on liver-coloured mud. Ahead of her the narrow beach was bounded by yellow rocks. She took stock of herself. Vomit had glued her hair to the side of her face and formed lumps on her eyelashes. The front of her nightie was stiff and below her waist it was plastered to her thighs by the sticky blood that also streaked her legs.

"Will I ever be clean again?" she wondered.

She decided to go in search of clean water inland.

When she tried to stand on them the bigger rocks crumbled under her feet like gigantic puff-balls and dissolved into sweet-smelling dust so that she started to choke again as she climbed. At the top she was disappointed to find that as far as they eye could see there was nothing but barren, dun-coloured fen with no feature but a few brown, scummy pools with yellow grass growing round them. Most of the land was too poisoned, however, even to support grass and it stretched before her for miles, flat, stark and empty. Only the occasional dead tree raised its branches from the marsh to supplicate or to threaten. Hesione crumpled on the fungus rock and wept.

She wept because she was fouled and could not get clean — because she was hungry and could not eat — because she was tired and could not rest — because she was weary and could not go home — but most of all she wept because she felt she deserved to be in this place. The only consolation she could find was that she would soon be dead of hunger and that way, at least, she would finally escape.

With sinking heart she struggled back over the rocks to the beach and walked out along the headland. Hoping she might see something encouraging from this vantage point she looked along the shoreline and saw, in the next bay, three hulking shapes lying on the mud. She hurried toward them with no high hopes that they would be alive, and was delighted when one of them turned its head toward the sound of her footsteps.

The clothing these creatures wore was dark brown, and for a moment she feared that they were the half-seal people. Then she saw that the face had none of the keen, gloating look of the selkies, but was wreathed in fat and seemed the picture of indolence. Black, heavy hair hung on either side of the fat-slabbed face; the eyes were like dirty thumb-prints in dough; the mouth and nose were tiny as if the creature had no use for the effort of breathing, or even eating. The chins rose straight from the bulging bosom and concealed the jaw, but on seeing Hesione the creature rolled over toward her and opened its mouth in a dainty yawn to show teeth like needles. It made no attempt to rise, but its chest heaved two or three times as it filled its lungs to speak. She had the impression it was not used to that function either. It wheezed,

"Well, look what we've got here."

At this the two others rolled over and six cloudy eyes fixed themselves on Hesione in faint curiosity. The one farthest from her started to shake. The quaking increased as she stared at it until it reached a climax and the creature burst out,

"Skinny little thing, isn't she?"

They all began to quake at once.

"Who are you?" enquired Hes, feebly.

There was a long silence while they brought their quaking under control and found their breath.

"Ectually," said the first one, mocking her, "we're sirens, aren't we girls?"

The one nearest to her giggled aloud — thin high and husky.

"That's right." she gasped, "You know, the kind that lure men to their doom by the beauty of their singing."

Hesione looked at them blankly.

"I know, I know," said the nearest one — speech seemed to be coming more easily to her now, "you're thinking that sirens are supposed to be beautiful in their persons as well as in their voices"

"No, really I..." Hes began politely, but the siren silenced her with a flap of her doughy hand.

"Believe me — there's more to sex-appeal than a pretty face and a cute body, isn't there, girls?"

The others quivered in mirthful agreement, and,

exhausted for the moment by their efforts, they sank back and closed their eyes.

After a decent interval Hesione turned away and began to clamber off over the fungus-rocks. The smell of the women was disgusting and she would have been pleased to get away from it, but somehow she was not optimistic. Sure enough, she had barely made it over the first two rocks when a voice like tearing fibre-glass reached her.

"Don't go, pet," — it was the first siren — "we don't see many new girls around here nowadays. Stay and give us your news."

"Yeah," agreed the next one, "you might decide to stay with us when you get to know us. We're a lot nicer than those snotty bitches in the West. You'll find that out."

"Shut up," wheezed the farthest one, "we don't want her around. There's not enough for us as it is."

"Shh," said the first, "we're not allowed to tell her. She has to decide for herself or it doesn't work."

Hesione hesitated. They were a form of company in this wasteland — the only form of company. She wondered what they meant by 'enough for us'. She could see nothing edible nearby, but perhaps there were fish in the water. She recoiled at the thought of eating anything from there.

"Anyway," struck up number two, "she's no danger to us. She doesn't know what she's doing."

"All the more reason to shut up and keep her in the dark. She might be a skinny little thing now, but who knows what magnificence she might grow to."

"Oh," said Hesione, "I'm no threat to you, I promise. I won't be here long, and I don't eat much. I've no appetite.."

The three sirens quaked and giggled.

"Is that right?" squeaked one, "I'm sorry to hear that."

"Take no notice of them," said the second, shifting her bulk to get a better view of Hes. "Tell us about yourself. Is it nice where you come from? Do you have fun? Do men find you attractive as well?"

"I think men find me attractive, but I couldn't say I enjoyed it."

The two others sniggered.

"Oh, you think men find you attractive, do you?" said one, "How do you know that? What have you got that other women haven't?"

"Nothing! Nothing, really. I take care of myself. I try to dress well, and some people say I'm pretty. I don't set out to be attractive. It just happens that way."

Laughter once more paralysed the women and reduced them to silent, helpless quivering.

"Ooooh," said one, wiping her eyes with a hand like an inflated rubber glove. "You don't put yourself out, do you? You're a great laugh, you are."

"Don't worry, pet," said three, "something as helpless as you will always pull them in. Don't you worry."

"But I don't want to pull them in — honestly."

One and two were heaving with mirth again, but three squinted up at Hes and said,

"You know, girls. I think she really believes all that crap. She really doesn't know what she's doing, or how she does it."

"Doing what?" grated Hes. She was getting tired of this teasing. "I can't do anything any other woman can — at least, not where I come from."

"D'you hear that?" skirled one. "Shite in a bucket! If they're all like her we're going to be overrun in no time."

"What do you mean?" Hes shouted, "What's so

special about the women in this place?"

"See — she doesn't know a thing. You're going to have to show her. I tell you, she's pig ignorant."

"Show her yourself, dear. You've got the best of any of us."

At this they all three squealed with laughter and Hesione had to wait till they regained control of their feeble respiration.

"Come over here, pet," said three at last.

With a sinking heart Hes approached. When she got near the woman leaned back on her vast ham-shaped arms, raised her knees and opened her legs. The dirty brown dress slid up her thighs to her groin and, horribly embarrassed, Hesione had to stare at the top of the woman's head to avoid the sight of her pudend.

"Come on, dearie. Have a good look," she said, jiggling her thighs impatiently.

"What?...There?!" said Hes hopelessly.

"Yes, there. What the Hell else should I mean?"

Squirming with dismay she let her eyes travel down the woman's legs to the vast, dingy thighs. There was so much fat hanging in folds that at first she could not make out the target area, then, with the blood pounded deafeningly in her ears, she saw the woman's vulva. At first glance it seemed normal, if somewhat inflamed, but the woman obligingly shifted her weight. Then Hesione saw that the whole area was a mass of writhing red tentacles. As her eyes glued themselves to the revolting sight she felt they must be filling her whole face. She was nothing but eyes, and there was nothing to see but the siren's vast and appalling cunt — its pink-tipped tentacles groping at the air, blindly, as if each one had a kind of will. Strangling on another wave of nausea, Hesione tore her eyes away and fled off along the beach. The siren's wheezing laughter followed her.

Running was hard on the clinging mud, and she had not gone far before she stumbled on some half-buried rocks. She fell, and as she fell she closed her eyes, hoping that she would open them in another place. She was disappointed to find on opening them that she was lying face down in the same mud, in the same landscape, but mercifully hidden from the sirens by a line of rocks. Cautiously she raised her head to peer over the rocks and saw something that brought her to her feet. A man was emerging from the sea.

He came out of the liquid in an awkward strut and made towards the sirens. His body and limbs were covered with the red slime, and his head was capped by some white mucous. He stopped and hailed the creatures, who didn't move. Their backs were toward her but Hes assumed they were watching his approach with the same indolence as they had her own. The man advanced to within about twelve feet of the nearest and paused again, staring at her.

Hesione was sure she should give some kind of warning, but didn't know how to frame it. It seemed absurd to warn a man agains the sight of the vile pudend, when it had done her no harm. She shut her mouth and sank against the rocks to watch.

The siren and the man studied each other — the man clearly not liking what he saw. Then she gave a sigh, sank onto her back in the mud and opened her legs as far as possible. Hesione bit her thumb as the man's eyes wandered reluctantly toward the siren's crotch. Then a change came over him, and the deepening frown of disgust was all at once replaced as his mouth grew slack and his eyelids drooped in a show of ecstasy. Hesione could hardly contain a scream as he dropped to his knees in front of the monster and, with a moan, began tearing at the zip in his trousers. She could not believe that what he had seen did not violently repel him, let alone attract him with such inexorable power. Yet the evidence was before her as he sank onto the siren with a sigh of pleasure. The siren grunted with satisfaction, wrapped her legs round him and, with astounding agility, rolled over on top of him. Hesione was left with nothing but the sight of her wide back.

Nevertheless she looked away with her stomach churning again and threatening to go into spasm. By and by her attention was drawn back to the creatures by a series of rythmical sounds. She tried to close her mind to it but it would not go away. It forced itself between the sealed edges of her ears. She shook her head to stop it penetrating, muttering, "Sick, sick, sick," but it did no good. The sounds came in a steady, rythmical, liquid sucking which, as she listened, increased in pace and intensity. Ragged thought flew across her brain.

"Sick — sick. I won't listen. I can't. It's horrible. It's nothing to do with me. Oh, God when will they finish? Can't I get away? They'll see me. Oh, dear sweet God, what are they doing? It's not sex. It's horrible — sickening. He wanted to do it! He wanted to touch her! How could he? He couldn't stop himself — not after he'd seen... It's nothing to do with me. Oh, God, what is she doing to him? He's an adult. He can make his own choices. What is she doing? Oh, sweet, merciful God. I know what she's doing. I know what it is. She's feeding off him!!"

And as the thought brought her screaming to her feet the sucking climaxed in a bubbling shout, and the man tore himself free. He stood beside the monster staring down at himself with horror. Hes saw that his whole abdomen from breastbone to groin was a gaping red hollow. Shreds of skin hung from the edges of the wound and blood and pus ran out. The man at last broke into a sob, and ran stumbling blindly past Hesione's refuge. Shreds of skin fell from him and lay

*pale against the mud. She went to pick them up as if
she could restore them to him and a voice behind her
squealed,*

*"There you go, dearie. Fancy a piece of him for
yourself, do you?"*

*Convulsively she threw the skin from her and
rounded on the siren. The one who had devoured the
man was leering at her, but the others were lying with
their eyes closed, as if asleep. The siren's face was
wreathed in a smile of repletion.*

*"YOU ARE DISGUSTING!" Hesione began, but
rage and loathing choked her.*

*"Oh, look at this, you two," jeered the siren to her
companions, "she's going to cry."*

*The others opened their eyes and snickered. Number
two said,*

"She's missed her chance and she's raging."

*"The only thing I want," snarled Hesione, "is the
means to destroy you. That's the only thing that will
give me pleasure, ever again!"*

*"OOOOOH!" shrieked the sirens and sank back in
the mud in mock terror. Hesione brought her hands up
to hide her face and saw that one still had a piece of
the man's skin sticking to it. She looked at it and
thought,*

"At least he will be revenged."

*The skin on her hand writhed, and began to grow.
Thicker and thicker and longer and longer it grew, and
as it grew it curled up on itself to form a tube. Once
it had become about two inches in bore it stopped
thickening and grew laterally until Hes found she was
holding a small fireman's hose of pale rubber with
narrow brass nozzle. At her mental command the
nozzle began to stream with fire and she turned it on
the sirens. One by one she ran the jet of red and yellow
fire onto the hulking bodies and watched them as they*

squirmed and blackened. Round and round she passed the fire, over each of them for a few seconds at a time and exulted in their shrieks of agony. Yet as soon as the fire passed off them each one began to laugh again. They sniggered and tittered and jeered at Hesione, unconcerned as their eyes melted and poured down their faces, their skin shrank and cracked open, and their hair blew away in threads of ash.

"Shut up!" screamed Hesione, "SHUTUPSHUTUP-SHUTUPSHUTUPSHUTUP!!!" and the fire poured over them.

But they would not be silent until they were reduced to smoking piles of slag lying in the mud. Then at her command the hose gave out a powerful jet of scalding, clean water and she scoured the last reeking ashes off the beach.

At last the final fragment of black bone was gone and she stopped, looked up and saw a purple sun standing high in the ochre sky. Like a labourer after a good morning's work, she rested her hands on her hips and looked at the clean beach.

"That takes care of you!" she said aloud.

And behind her someone chuckled.

She turned and saw a small group of selkies watching her from the rocks.

"That takes care of you," repeated one, mockingly. "That takes care of you. I wonder who'll take care of you. I wonder, wonder who?"

The others joined the barrage.

"You're so good at taking care of things!"

"She cares for things so well."

"She coddles them to death."

"I hope she never takes care of me!"

"Infanticide."

"Midwife."

"Murderer."

"Monster."

"Who's going to look after her?"

"She needs looking after."

"She's a babe in arms."

"What do you do with babies?"

"You know what she did with our babies."

"Choked them."

"Burned 'em."

"Drowned 'em."

"The sirens?" gasped Hes, "They weren't your babies."

"She's telling us..."

"..they weren't our babies."

"Nothing to worry about, then."

"It's okay."

"It's okay."

"It's our turn, now."

"We'll take care of you. Don't worry, pet. You're our pet now. We'll take care of you."

They had been closing on her as they spoke, and now, suddenly, they pounced. They surrounded her and bore her to the ground.

"Dinner time," sang one, and the others chimed in. "DINNERTIME!!"

Her head was siezed and forced back, bony fingers were driven between her teeth and her mouth pulled open. They were almost standing on top of her, their gloating faces intent. She tried not to struggle and give them the pleasure they were anticipating, but her resolution failed when she saw what they were bringing toward her mouth.

"NO!!!" she roared past the fingers in her mouth.

The selkies chortled. She twisted her head away and bit down on the fingers. Her tongue was scratched as the fingers were pulled out but she clamped her mouth *shut and drew a big breath. To her surprise all the selkies stepped back and let her fall.*

"Don't damage our fingers. We haven't had them long."

"We're very proud of our fingers."

They shook their heads.

"Well," said one of the men. "It looks as if she doesn't want to be a hag, after all."

"Hah!" said one of the women, "she's half-way to being one already. The change has started, and we couldn't stop it now if we wanted to."

"...which we don't."

Hesione lay back and squeezed her eyes shut. She felt the fungus-rock beneath her begin to crumble and give way, and to her relief she began to fall back into her own world.

She awoke lying beside James. His breathing was regular and his sleep untouched by the struggle she had just gone through. She reviewed as much of the dream as she dared, then gave thanks that she was home. Disturbed by her movements James rolled over and threw his arm across her. In misery she realised that her lochia had finished, her baby was very easy to manage, and the six week's post-partum was over. Soon she would have to return to normal marital duties. The thought made her press her thighs together and roll onto her side away from him as, for the first time, she felt actively sickened at the idea. Tears trickled across the bridge of her nose and dripped onto the pillow.

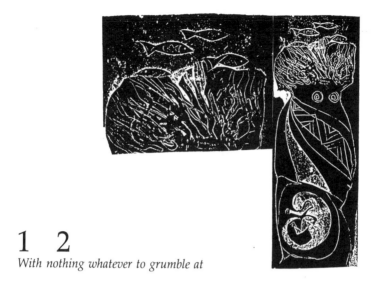

1 2
With nothing whatever to grumble at

Hesione took her first ever trip alone with the children. She had been sitting with James over breakfast when suddenly he turned to her and said,

"Why don't you take the car today? You could go round the coast with the kids." He warmed to the idea. "You could take a picnic. It's a smashing day — far too good to stick indoors — and there won't be many more of them this year."

She couldn't quite make out what he was saying. She had been fixing the day's plans in her head as she now did every day. If she arranged things carefully in her mind she had found that she could keep the shadows in her mind from swelling up at her. But before she started the day she had to learn the plan off by heart — reciting it like a mantra — so that when things started to slip through she could at once sweep the fabric across and curtain them from herself. James repeated his offer and she turned a dazed face toward him.

"I can get a lift to work," he was saying, "with Alistair, and you could have the car all day. You're in the house to much with the kids. You never go anywhere and it's not good for you. Remember what your mother said."

"What's that?"

"She said bored mothers make bored children."

"I'm not bored."

"Not yet, maybe, but you soon could be. When did you last spend an afternoon with Karen, even?

"I don't like the taste of vodka."

"Or Charlotte?"

"She's far too busy to waste time with me."

"Or anywhere but here?"

"I don't really have the time."

"You've just got out of the habit. You used to make time for outings with Robin. You even took him to your keep fit classes. When did you last go to them?"

She blinked at him.

"What do you want me to do?" she asked in resignation.

"Look, I don't want you to do anything special. I just think you ought to have a change of scene. You're getting slack. If I were you I would grab at the chance to take a wee picnic. I know I'm not you — but you should make some effort."

"Well, I'll have to tidy up first. I can't go out and leave the sitting-room like that."

"The room looks fine. All you have to do is go into the garage, get the car out and drive off. You don't even have to fill the tank — I did it yesterday."

She looked into the sitting-room. There were books on the floor beside James's chair, an opened newspaper lay on the coffee table beside two unwashed cups and the ornaments on the mantlepiece had got into the wrong order again.

"I have to put things into the right places," she explained, "or else the wind will get in."

As she spoke she was picturing it. The corner of the newspaper would start to flutter because it wasn't folded; the leaves of the books would fly open if the books weren't shelved; and with such heavy things as candlesticks in disarray the wind would be very strong. She shivered.

"What a notion," said James, laughing, and went to phone Alistair.

He had made up their mind. Hesione dutifully went to the kitchen cupboard and pulled the cool-box from the bottom shelf. As she did so it occurred to her that a change had taken place. In times past she had been the one to organise his leisure for him. Saturday mornings had been agony for her because he couldn't decide what to do and would loaf about till lunch-time and she would grow impatient and frustrated. In theory she thought that if she respected him she would not want to tell him what to do; in practice her respect had its limits. She had found ways of prompting him, by nudging conversation into fruitful channels, or by rummaging about in the hall cupboard until the tools for a certain project were lying where he could not but see them, or, finally, by bustling about herself so hard that he had to get moving or be buffeted by her slipstream. She would certainly not have chivvied him as he was now doing her, nor would she have given him verbal instructions about how to fill his time.

"It begins to look as if someone's made a switch. I'll have to look into this."

James called goodbye and left by the front door.

"No kiss," she muttered. "I suppose they could have done it while I was in hospital. What should I do?"

She drove along the coast road round the foot of the golden-brown hills — past the towering steel of naval installations — and on, out to where living went on at a gentler pace. Robin watched out for 'Fiss' and 'Tees' and other nameable objects until the rythmical movement made him nod off. Beside him, in her own small seat, Neri slept soundly. Neither of them moved when she pulled up near a picnic spot they had discovered that summer. She got out and walked over to the rocks thinking,

"They'd better have their sleep out. I can do with a moment of peace."

A pair of eyes like black beads appeared in a crevice in the rocks and a large claw beckoned to her. It was the hermit crab. She followed it and slipped into a crack that widened smoothly to admit her. Unconcerned by this remarkable thing she hurried after the crab and found herself in a cavern so vast that the walls and ceiling were hidden in darkness. On the far side of the cavern she could see a large angular building whose nearest corner jutted at her like the prow of a ship. The sides were studded with rows of lights like portholes, each row containing hundreds of lights. But, big as it was, it was dwarfed in the huge cavern and the all the lights illuminated only a small part of its area.

As they neared the building she could see that every second row of lights lit a railed walkway running along the outside of the block. Little doors with round windows opened onto the walkways. Closer to, the block looked even more like a ship. Hesione waited for someone to appear and hail them.

"It could be a block of flats, I suppose, but the flats would be tiny. They have to be cabins on a deck."

She turned to the crab to ask him about it but he was studying an anemone balanced on his claw. He said,

"Unthink suburbsurd," and his eyes swivelled away from her.

"I'm sorry,"

"Sorry, schmorry," muttered the crab.

"I'm on my own, then."

There was no reply. She advanced smartly on the housing block and started to look for a way in. Rounding a corner she came upon a brightly lit flight of concrete stairs.

"Not a lot of help — but it's a start. Maybe I'm in a car-park after all."

She made her way up the stairs and found the entrance to each floor was closed by a metal studded door with letters stencilled on it. When she came to the floor marked P-Q she pushed at the door and was surprised to find it opened easily in spite of its weight. Her guide had disappeared so with a mental shrug she set off along the balcony.

The first cabin door was locked and there was a curtain over the window. She tried to peer through but could only see a few shadowy shapes. The next door was locked also, but she could see in through a gap in the curtain. Inside there was a life-sized diorama of a family kitchen and it was not immediately obvious that the people were immobile. The woman at the stove stood with a pan in her hand poised over the hob; the children sat at the table frozen over a jigsaw; the husband slumped in his chair, inert, with a newspaper in front of his face. Only the dog — caught in the act of leaping up for attention — gave any sign of ever being animated.

She went to the next door and looked in through the window without trying the lock. The room was brightly lit, but all she could see was some expensive, ugly modern furniture and a mound of slimy brown rock. There was a notice thumb-tacked to the door which said

'An Englishman's Home is His Castle'. She sighed and moved on.

The next door, labelled 'In the Spring a Young Man's Fancy' revealed a small room covered in pictures of cars and racing drivers with an incongruous red velvet sofa shaped like a heart, and on it another heap of slimy rock.

She continued along the row finding every door locked and inside only darkness, tedious dioramas or cryptic heaps of rock. Finally she found an unlocked door which she at once opened and entered. She found herself in a corner of a room painted white. The furniture — two chairs and a narrow bed — was also white, as were the curtains. The only inhabitant was a young girl, about fourteen, partially encased in brown rock. On her left side the rock had encroached only as far as her left armpit, but on the right side it had reached her neck. If it were not for the fact that her colour was good she could have been taken for dead. There was no sign of breath in her body and her long hair, trapped in the rock, did not move in the air current from the door. The bubbling brown slime of the rock seemed to be taking her whole weight and she leaned against it, her eyes closed and a faint smile on her plump little mouth. Hesione leaned as close to the child as she dared without touching the rock and heard no sound of breathing. A wisp of her own hair trailed across her cheek but brought no response. She studied the tender curve of the cheek, the neat pink mouth and the freckles scattered like pollen across the long, narrow nose and at last she recognised the child. Then she felt very lonely indeed.

She hurried out to find the hermit crab. Even his sarcastic presence would be a comfort at that point. To her surprise he was standing just outside the door.

"What am I to do?" she begged him.

"Whatabout?"

"I mean about...that poor child in there, of course. She's trapped in that rock or coral, or whatever. We have to get her free."

"Whoosez?"

"I do. She's caught and can't move — and she's stopped breathing. We'll have to rescue her."

"Shyupset?" enquired the crab.

"Well, no. She looks very serene, if it comes to that. But that's not the point."

The crab's eyes tracked up and down her body insultingly.

"Look," said Hes, beginning to get exasperated, " — she's not breathing, and she's not moving. If we don't get her out of the stuff it will grow right up and cover her. That must be what's happened to others here."

"So?"

"So?!! Goddammit, that's me in there. You can be as cynical as you like but I don't relish being smothered in that brown muck."

The crab stopped staring at her and minced past her through the door. She followed him and they both looked at the child as she reclined against her tube of rock. For the first time she noted creatures moving about in the slime and she shuddered hysterically.

"What is that filthy stuff all round her?" she demanded, "and what are those things... moving."

"A-crabs, life-limpets," his shell bobbled, "mind-coral."

"How can I get her out of it?"

"Why?"

"She has to be free," she cried, fizzing with chagrin. "Can't you see — she's not breathing."

The crab's shell bobbled again and he drew his claw inside. The shell settled down until it rested on the floor and only his eyes could be seen peering up at her *from under the rim.*

"I'm sorry to shout," said Hes rapidly, "but it's not easy to keep calm when you see yourself trapped. I promise not to lose my temper again."

"Suburbsurd," he repeated impassively.

"Alright — I'm absurd," snapped Hesione, "I'll try and improve."

She woke with a jolt. The low-angled autumn sun was shining directly in her face and for a while she was confused. It was clear she had not been asleep for long for her children had not stirred.

"I must have sat down for a minute and dozed off," she concluded. "I wish that dratted crab would be a little more enlightening."

On looking about her she decided that this rocky hollow was not a good place to bring the baby. She climbed back into the car and drove along to a small, disused harbour they had seen but never had the chance to visit before. There was a good parking bay with a seat beside it and a fair stretch of clean shingle for Robbie to scratch in. A crumpled wooden pier leaned negligently into the water and nearby stood a small stone building with a red roof and lobster pots stacked beside the door. A black and white sheepdog lay panting on the shady side of the house. It was quiet and sunny here in a way that made you think it had always been quiet and sunny.

The children slept on. Hes leaned her arms on the steering-wheel and brushed her mouth against them so that the fine hairs tickled her lips. Her mind drained itself.

A brown-flecked gull landed on the side of the pier — a baby herring-gull. It was a sad, dingy thing beside the spanking white of the adults squabbling in the bay.

Awkwardly it shifted from foot to foot and reared and ducked its head, piping miserably.

Five minutes passed. the gull was silent, huddled down its feathers. A vast red jelly-fish sucked at the surface, found nothing and made off with a weary squirm. The dingy young gull started to whistle and crane again and it was joined by another youth who started to whistle and beg also.

"Go and find your own fish!" thought Hesione. "Lazy little things, you should have learned to fend for yourselves by now."

An adult flew over in disgust at their maudlin racket and landed between them. The two dingy babies sidled toward each other — two steps at a time — whistling and craning and ducking to peer at each other between the adult's legs. The adult stared fiercely at nothing in particular. The young ones got closer and closer — the adult stood its ground but they sidled nearer — three feet, then two, then eighteen inches. The adult toppled off the pier with an unhappy 'awk' and wheeled overhead to regather its dignity. The whistling stopped.

Hesione laughed aloud.

"Those horrid little clowns. I bet they had it all planned. I must tell Jamie about it when we get back."

At the sound of her voice the children began to stir so she slipped out to get the food from the boot. When she got back Robin was rubbing his eyes with the heels of his hands.

"You do that just like your father," she told him.

"Dink," he said, and she handed him his cup from the cool box.

"Would you like to do this again," she asked him as he gulped his orange juice. "I don't suppose you care, but I would like to. It's lovely and quiet. What am I doing talking to you like this? Oh, well, why not? There's no-one to hear me, and ma says I should talk to you more than I do."

They ate lunch while a gentle breeze blew in through the window. The gulls circled over the harbour, mewing and quarrelling. A man went into the house with the red roof. The dog got up, scratched and followed him.

"Wouldn't it be nice to live in that wee house?" she asked Robin.

"'Ouse," he agreed.

"No-one would bother us — we could do just what we felt like."

Neri snuffled and woke but Hes calmly finished her lunch. It wasn't until the baby made a prolonged buzzing that her mother lifted her from her seat.

"Us old ones need time to ourselves, don't we, Robbie?" she said and fed the baby a cool feed without a qualm.

"Look at that — I used to go daft trying to get your feed to just the right temperature — of course mother said 'the right milk is always at the right temperature', but sister did say it's okay to feed a young baby with cool milk as long as its body's warm. Imagine me sitting here with my clothes all over the place...

"Anyway, breast-fed babies fill their nappies at every feed. Yech! I couldn't stand it!"

She whisked the dispo off Neri and replaced it with another.

"Nothing to it," she said, and swabbed her hands with an antiseptic wipe.

"Dink," Robin answered, waving his cup.

"You're getting bored," she told him, and released him to scrabble in the stones.

He seemed amused so she took Neri and walked along the roadway a few yards to where she could see the other side of the pier. There she found the sea freighted with a mass of rotting weed, plastic bottles and bits of orange rope. The thick weed rubbed itself against the timbers of the pier and damped down the motion of the waves to a slow, treacly heaving. And hanging upside down on the surface was a big, white pram. She ran back to Robbie and scooped him out of the shingle. He protested and fought against her as she strapped him in the car. Neri started buzzing again.

"I'm sorry," said Hes to their angry little faces, "but it's not clean here. I'm sorry."

She got them home in record time.

1 3

Be to her virtues very kind; Be to her faults a little blind

For the next few days Hester moved very slowly. The short period of calm she had enjoyed with her children lay in her head like a crystal bowl full to the brim. If she moved abruptly she might spill some of its pure contents, or even shatter the bowl. Then one afternoon, well before his usual time, James appeared in the doorway of the sitting-room, his faced glowing with pleasure.

"What are you doing home," she asked, deliberately.

"There was nothing more for me to do," he answered, slightly offended at his tepid reception. "We've finished the Korean contract and it was too late in the day to start a whole new ball-game so I came home. I thought you'd be pleased."

"I am," she said, and nodded slowly, waiting for the rest of his news. He paused then went on,

"I had a chat with Cameron this afternoon, and he said it would be alright for me to work on this next job in the house. My office is getting painted and I'd have to share with Peter Doyle. It's not that I mind him, but I prefer to work on my own, and then I thought of my drawing-board in the loft collecting dust — you know, the good one my folks got me for my twenty-first — so I spoke to him and he said he doesn't mind where I work, as long as the work's done. So I can work at home."

He was grinning from ear to ear. Hesione stared at him, not sure how to tell him she couldn't understand a word. He seemed as pleased as a dog with two tails, but everything he had said had tangled in her brain and she couldn't find the right response. His grin was fading.

"I can work in the house," he repeated, slowly as if she were stupid, " — in the spare room — and I can spend more time with you and the kids."

"You want to work in the house — here — as if it was the office?"

"Yes," he replied, "do you have any objections?"

"No, none — Neri needs no room."

"Oh, is that what's the matter with you? Don't worry about that," he said airily, "we'll be gone from here by the time Neri needs a room of her own."

"Where will we have moved to?"

"Somewhere better than this. We always planned to, didn't we? I reckon this place is well worth 70K by now. We could move out of town. You always wanted to."

She nodded vigorously in agreement only to shut him up. He was flooding the room with all these threatening novelties. It was taking her all her time to cope with routine reality, let alone thrust herself into a seething cauldron of change. Her eyelids felt hot and sore.

"Shall I put the car away for you," she offered, keen to get away from him and clear her head up again.

"I'll do that," he chirped. "You'll be wanting to get tea for the kids." At the door he stopped and said, "You do think it's a good idea, don't you?"

"Yes, of course. It'll be wonderful."

He scampered off, pleased, but she was still confused. She watched him from the window as he locked the garage, and waited for him to wave to the crowd of small dark people walking up the hill toward him. Three of the men were carrying a net on their shoulders, and some carried long black clubs in their thumbless hands. The women hurried up the hill behind them, some carrying white bundles in their arms and all had that intent look which meant someone was for it. They approached the house and passed it without so much as a glance at James, who ignored them in his turn.

"They must have been sent for someone else, this time," Hes concluded.

The following Friday Hester and James went out to dinner. She wasn't pleased to be going, natch, but flabby Ron had put it to them as a chance to meet their new neighbours and make them welcome. She had to accept or she would have looked cheap. She could at least hope to keep clear of Ron's implacable groping because the thrash was due to take place in the local Chinese.

"I've booked a table for eight," said Ron, "and you buggers had better turn up. There's no point in trying to do it at home, Karen's such a lousy cook — God knows how I got to be the shape I am — it wouldn't be a welcome for the poor sods. More of a threat, if you take my meaning."

They took his meaning and turned up at five past eight. They didn't have to search for their party when they got there since Ron was sitting at the big table in the window in deafening beach-shirt. Hes got out of the car with the usual sinking feeling as he waved and hooted through the glass. James, on the other hand, was feeling good about things. He patted her bum as they walked through the porchway of plastic bamboo tiles and said,

"You're putting on the beef, dear. 'Bout time you went back to squash on a Wednesday."

"Is that right?" said Hes, "It's a good job we came here for dinner, then. The smell of MSG makes me puke."

"Oh aye," said James, "where's the wee petted lip then."

"Right here, under the wee thinning nostrils."

"You're in a helluva mood."

"You got it," she said, and marched over to the table brushing aside the waiter who was offering to show her to it. Ron was acting petulant.

"What's the matter with you two, then," he demanded. "I was waving like a loony at you as you came in and you ignored me."

This was her cue to blush and stammer sorry.

"Don't be a moron, Ron," she said.

The company gaped at her. We were beginning to enjoy the evening. Karen, the empty glasses in front of her testifying to her good humour, laughed. Hes winked at her.

"If you want to know the truth, honey, James was being rude about the size of my bum. Just because he's dessiccated, he thinks it makes him superior somehow."

Even Karen had a bit of a problem laughing at this, but the other two took up the struggle.

"James, Hester," said Ron, grabbing centre-stage back, "meet Sammy and Lorna."

"Sammy and Lorna what?" enquired Hes.

"What?"

"I take it they have a surname."

Karen wriggled a bit. I told Hes to watch it. She was beginning to sound like her mother on a bad day. She promised to take it down a point.

"McLeish," offered Sammy along with his hand.

"How do you do?" she said, surprised when he stood up. We looked at him. He had the bland, good looks that you find in spectacle adverts. We realised with a slight sense of panic that we would not recognise him again. He pulled out the chair next to Ron for her.

"Shit!" she said to me.

The woman on the other side of Ron was expensively dressed with the kind of carelessness that only requires one minute in three spent looking in a mirror. It must be Lorna.

"Hi," she said and moved her hand a bit. We decided it must the four gold chains on her wrist that was weighing her down and keeping her from being polite. You have to feel sorry for someone under a burden like that. Ron slipped a hot, damp hand round Hes's waist and squeezed.

"Well, isn't this nice," he breathed.

"If you say so, Ron," she said, leaning toward him intimately.

"Oh, I do — I do," he crooned, staring down her cleavage.

"Fine," she said quietly. We didn't want to get thrown out just yet. "I'll enjoy myself too if you don't let your hands wander, there's a good boy. Perhaps Lorna would appreciate your attention. She's supposed to be the guest of honour, isn't she?"

Ron turned to Lorna reluctantly. She didn't look as if she would rise to his baiting like Hes used to. She didn't look as if she was breathing.

"Where did she get that awful yellow tan," Hes asked me, "— in a supermarket?"

She caught James's eye and winked at him. He shook his head slightly and sat down beside Karen.

"Po-faced bugger," I said.

We sat in silence while they ordered and ate the first course. Sammy had a fine easy small talk. He was obsessed with performance cars and when he heard James was currently driving a Ford saloon he wrote him out of the conversation. Hes found herself at the receiving end of some heavy appraisal.

"What's he going to do," she asked me, " — take out insurance?"

"You're looking good tonight," I warned her.

"So? The nerve of men. Here I've struggled to keep James at bay for weeks, and he thinks he's just going to climb aboard."

"Maybe he thinks you're too zippy for your Ford-driving husband."

"Hah!"

Her eyes wandered over to the partition hiding the kitchen entrance. It was fitted with a large fish-tank and she stared at them to avoid being drawn into the conversation, but Sammy leaned across to her confidingly.

"Do you like fish?" he asked.

"Yes," she lied, to see what would happen. "Do you?"

"Good." He leaned back as if he had made a conquest. "You must come to one of my salons in town. I have hundreds of tropical fish in tanks there."

"Except they keep dying," said Lorna.

"What a charming idea," said Hes ambiguously. "I'd love to come, but to tell the truth I was looking at the coral. Star Coral, it's called, and a lovely example."

"Oh, you know about marine life, then?" he said, fixing an interested smile in place.

"Not really. After my father died my mother kept his

library intact. I spent a lot of time browsing — picking up bits and pieces — no serious study, I'm afraid."

Sammy smiled brilliantly at her. He had noted the mention of a library.

"Sam keeps the fish tanks because he read somewhere it would keep his customers mesmerised," said his wife. "He reckons if they get calm enough they won't see what a mess the stylists have made."

You could tell they were a devoted couple.

"I didn't think that mattered nowadays," said Ron, clambering back into the conversation. "I thought modern styles were designed to look as messy as possible."

"That's just the teeny-boppers," said Lorna, smoothing down her own sleek dye-job. "The rest of us still have some taste."

"I can see you do," said Ron grinning wolfishly. Lorna gave him the nearest thing to a smile she had managed all evening.

"Oh, boy," said Hes to me, "he's making a conquest."

Sammy cut in.

"Those modern — 'messy' — styles take a great deal of know-how. If the stylist doesn't know his job it looks Goadawful."

"...as opposed to just awful," added Lorna.

Everybody squirmed except Hes. Sammy admired her self-control, or did he think it was anæsthesia? He leaned over her again, drenching her in a waft of his aftershave.

"I hope you will come to our Salon. I would love to see that ash-blonde in a really good cut. Who do you go to here?"

"As a matter of fact, James does it with the hedge-clippers," said Hes, looking at her husband, "don't you, dear?"

James looked appalled. Karen choked on her vodka.

"Where's the main course?" she went on. "We might as well get it over with."

Sammy was silent. He seemed to have decided she was more than he could handle. Ron tried to smooth things over.

"Yeah, we ordered hours ago. Where's that bloody wee waiter?"

"They'd have to roast the duck specially," said Sammy doing his foodie number. "We should have known we'd have to wait. Why don't we have another drink to pass the time?"

Rebuked, but not chastened, Hes looked round the restaurant. The lighting was dim to hide the customers from each other. But the light in the fish tanks was brilliant. The streams of bubbles glittered and life in there seemed real and vivid, the action swift, the inhabitants distinguished. All in all what went on in the tanks was a groove beside what was going on in the restaurant. The humans all seemed half-finished and aimless.

"We came here, supposed to enjoy ourselves," she said to me. "And look what happens — all we do is sit and try to score off each other. Everyone pulling in different directions and clouding up their own purposes like squids squirting ink. Does anyone know what they're doing here?"

"No. But they all think they do," I told her, "which is worse."

Around her the conversation had all but died and her companions were flapping their arms at the waiter to try and get more wine. We thought such dedicated corporate effort should have a higher aim. She got tired of all the waiting and took herself to the Ladies. Once she was in there she caught sight of herself in the mirror.

"Christ," she said, "James is right, you know. I am putting on the beef."

At that point I took off. I can't take it when she starts banging on about her looks.

On her way back to the table she stopped by the fish. Indifferent to her face so close to them they went about their business. They flicked and glided in and out of fronds and streams of bubbles; they hung above the bottom of clean crushed shells; they flew around coral cliffs. And yet Hesione couldn't shake off the feeling that what she was seeing was a charade — a display put on for the watching humans — and that what really mattered to them was hidden — encoded in what they did. It was a dance which was a set of signs for something else.

One of the tanks held assorted carp — gold, gold and black, black and red — and one white one. The white one fascinated her and seemed curious about her in return. She watched it as it swam round the tank and back to the glass on her side. It hung inspecting her two inches from her nose and she saw that its skin was translucent. Through the skin she could make out the rythmical twitching of its heart, the food sliding down its gullet and the fæces waiting in the colon.

"How horrible," she thought. "Not the slightest privacy for it — ever. I bet the lights don't even go off at night. I would hate to be like that. Maybe it's the paleness that makes it transparent. The others are all opaque."

Experimentally she slipped her hand up under the partition and poked her fingers in the water. Sure enough the light did shine through her skin, but her mass was too great for it to penetrate deeper than the dermis. The secrets of her skeleton would be kept.

"Hester!" came a voice behind her, "what the hell are you doing?"

She turned and found James glaring at her.

"This fish," she indicated weakly, " — you can see right through her."

Suddenly she became aware that everyone in the restaurant was staring at her. Some were amused; some, like Sammy, were disgusted. James took her arm.

"Don't make me go back to them," she whispered. "I want to go home. Please take me home."

"Don't talk daft," said James, "You'll come back and finish your meal."

She looked down at the hand on her arm and saw that his thumb was lying at a very strange angle. It had probably been grafted on. She looked up into his dark-brown eyes.

"This has gone too far," she thought. "It's time I did something about it. Only who's going to tell me what?"

1 4
Full fathom five thy father lies

Hesione never spent time in the hall unless it was unavoidable. Sometimes the door to the sea was there, and sometimes it was not, and when it was there she was afraid she would go through it. She had no intention of going, but in the same way a person with vertigo knows that if they look down from a height they will fall, she knew that if the door kept appearing, one day she would go through it. She also knew Nerine shared her danger.

At night, awake as usual, she lay listening to the wind savagely buffeting the house. She knew where it came from. It came through the door downstairs where torches flickered and the sea boomed and voices whispered and bubbled all night long. She had to get away from the door — she and the baby. Once they were well away from it she could think and plan and find help to get rid of it. If she could get away from the voices she might be able to sleep. Her eyes were so sore — they'd been sore for months. If she could sleep then her eyes would stop hurting and she would be safe because she wouldn't be able to see the selkies and their bulging eyes.

The weekend after the visit to the restaurant Hesione felt James watching her like a cat at a mousehole. She did her best to act like her old, quiet self, and hoped he didn't notice that she kept leaving lights on and doors open and turning the television up loud to cover the other sounds. The weather was bad and they all had to stay indoors. James pretended to be reading, but got very cross with her when she sneaked out one time with the baby wrapped in a shawl to try and get some peace for them. He announced that the weather wasn't fit for the baby to go out in the pram, let alone in nothing more than a blanket. This rage left her in a panic, but she remembered that he would have to leave the house, willy, nilly. Monday was coming and he had a meeting somewhere with the client for the lighter he was designing. He couldn't miss that.

Sunday night was bad. When she dozed off her blood began to thicken and squelch in her ears, and she would snap herself awake to find her vision blurred and her limbs stiff. She was sure that she must stay awake or her heart beat and breathing would almost vanish. Once or twice she got out of bed and paced up and down the landing but the noises from beyond the door drove her back to bed.

Soon after James had left the door appeared. Without giving way to her panic she dressed the children, packed a bag for Neri and left the house. Robin was left with Mrs MacAuley with the excuse that she had to take Neri to the clinic, and she took off before her neighbour could recall that the clinic was on Tuesday. At last she began to feel a shimmer of hope.

She hurried down the hill, her daughter bundled in her arms and the bag of feeding bottles and nappies banging on her hip. The day was cloudy but the cloud was high and a fresh wind flowed past her as she sped along. Grey houses below her and grey clouds above rushed to meet at a vanishing point in the sea.

Once at the coast road she hesitated for a moment then, in the distance, she saw someone perched on the railing at the edge of the promenade. As she approached them she became increasingly sure that it was Mrs MacCrimmond. Her heart was pounding and her pace was slowing in spite of her best efforts. The wind blew full into her body and she wrapped her arms round the baby to protect her from the battering. The sound of her heart nearly drowned out the wind as she forced herself against it toward the little woman. She pulled her head down and hunched her shoulders.

"You won't stop me that easily," she shouted, "I've had enough of your damn nonsense! I'll pay what I owe — I'll do what I have to do, but after that you are going to leave me alone!"

Suddenly all was silent. Mrs MacCrimmond sat in front of her on the white, rust-streaked railing with her back to the beach. She was wearing her brown skin coat. Her sallow, freckled face was crestfallen, resentful and sly.

"Right," snapped Hesione, " — tell me what to do."

"I don't know anything," the woman whined, "I'm just a messenger."

"Don't talk rubbish. You made my eyes smart with that ointment. You can tell me how to stop it — or lead me to someone who can."

"I'm not a power in any land. I pass between the three kingdoms freely, that's all."

"Which three kingdoms? What are you talking about?"

"I can't tell you anything. They would kill me on the spot if I tried to."

"Then I'm sorry for you, because either way you are going to die. If you don't tell me what I want to know I swear I will kill you with my bare hands. For the first time in my life I am angry and I don't care what happens to me. I am going to use that rage; I am going to protect my child from you and your nasty friends and, even though it may destroy me, I am not going to give up.

"Where do I get help?" she said, and stepped forward raising her fist.

The little woman smiled a slight, jeering smile saying,

"Then I wish you luck in your quest, for you will be doing something few have ever done before and survived. I have warned you. Now it is up to you."

"What do I have to do?"

"You must keep going along the shore till you come to the big rock pool at the headland. Then you sit there and wait till he comes."

"Who is he? How will I know him?"

"You will know him when you see him, but perhaps not at once. No-one else will be able to. When he sees that you have recognised him he will try to escape, and when he does you must be sure to keep him. He will try to shake you off by changing shape then you must take care not to yield to fear or to pain, and you must keep hold of him no matter what. The last shape he will take will be one of the seal kind and when he does that you must trap him with this rope of fish-gut. Once you have bound him with it he will have to take you where you need to go."

From her pocket she pulled a rope of white, rubbery stuff and pushed it into Hesione's hand.

"Where will he take me?"

"You will see for yourself. I cannot tell you, for I never passed the first test, myself."

All at once Hesione noticed there were tears in the woman's eyes.

"What are you telling me? The man will come, won't he?"

"Oh yes, he will come. The rock pool is his doorway

into the middle kingdom, and he must come. All you have to do is wait — and hold him. But I've already said too much."

All at once the wind skirled. Mrs MacCrimmond teetered on her perch and jumped off.

"I must go," she said and ran off with the wind behind her.

Hesione looked at the rubbery rope she had left.

"Well at least she won't bother me again," she said, and tucked the rope in her pocket.

The tide was well out leaving long reaches of bare shingle. Far off at the headland she could see white spray flying against the grey rocks, but the wind drowned the noise. Turning into the wind she set off in search of the rock pool. She lost all sense of time passing as she battled on like a tug-boat in a heavy sea. The wind was her enemy; it was a great snake circling the earth; it was a waterfall pouring onto her as she stumbled along; it was a rubber wall she must keep pushing against, for if she were to relax for even an instant it would spring back and throw her all the way back to the beginning of the day.

At last she realised she must be near her destination. The wind gave a terrible scream and flung itself at her so that she was driven back a few paces. Almost bent double, she renewed her attack. The sun came out and tried to dazzle her. She kept her face averted and turned down the beach cursing her enemies.

"Oh, no, you don't," she snarled, " — you won't catch me like that. I'm up to your little tricks, now."

In spite of her defiance she nearly passed the rock pool before she realise it was there. It lay in a huge rectangle of basalt that ran out into the sea and it was surrounded by dead, white weed. Nothing grew in the middle and she could see the bottom where the fine sand glinted.

"Nothing grows in really clean water," she mused.

She put the bag down and sat on the flat rock between the pool and the sea. Carefully she put the baby across her lap and made them comfortable. The wind had dropped and now it thrummed gently in her ear. She gazed out over the shifting sea and fell slowly into a torpor. Her body cooled, her heart slowed and the beat of her thickening blood began to toll like a tocsin. Her vision clouded and her hearing began to sharpen so that she could pick out the sound of each stone as the sea threw it onto the rocks.

"Damn!" she said, becoming aware of her state. "They can still get at me."

The baby whimpered a little so she took out a feeding bottle. Then, to make sure the child was warm, she opened her coat and held her against her body while she fed.

"There," she said, triumphant. "an animal wouldn't do this. I must do everything as human as possible — use all my faculties — use both eyes, and not on peripheral vision. What do I see when I look straight ahead and use both eyes?

"Patches of sunshine all around, playing on the sea. And the sea itself. Mussels like jet beads — the swing and draw of the waves on the rocks — sudden waterfalls appearing — barnacles like parchment creased and folded to make lampshades — volcanoes. The wind pulls strings of hair across my face. My eye's orbit frames the horizon. Behind me on the beach lie long brown straps of kelp. In the sky, the gulls are staggering on the wind. My nails are like pink shells. No — I am human, through and through. I am the one who sees and remembers these things — and I give them meaning."

A long time passed while Hesione sat looking and thinking — using words and making images. The baby woke again and was fed and changed. Hesione told her all about what she had seen and how she was not to worry about it because she had come to fix it.

"Whatever happens now I'm doing for you so that you will be able to sleep peacefully. It's a terrible thing, not being able to sleep. I hope it never happens to you. Or if it does you'll be able to deal with it promptly, before it gets to this stage."

The baby smiled at her explanation. Hesione put her over her shoulder and walked the few paces up and down the rock until she went to sleep. Then she sat down to resume her sea watch. The tide had turned back toward her.

As the early evening drew on she saw a group of people approaching along the beach. The looked like ordinary humans, but she watched them closely to be sure they were. To her amazement she recognised her husband, mother and sister in the group.

"Blast —" she thought, "I don't want them getting involved in this. Maybe if I keep quiet they'll understand that I have to be left alone and go away again."

Deliberately she turned her back on them and stared out over the sea. The little party stopped about twenty yards away and looked at her warily. They put their heads together and spoke quietly for a moment, then James broke away from the group and came to her.

"Hester!" he called gently. She ignored him so he tried harder,

"Hester, it's getting cold out here. You're going to get pneumonia if you stay sitting on those rocks. Why don't you come home? You can always come back in the morning if you want to."

What he said was true. It would soon be night and she was already feeling the chill. But what if the enemy came at sunset? She would have to stay till then, at least.

"Hester!" It was James again. "At least let me take the baby. She'll get her death of cold out here." He held out his arms.

"No!" she replied, shrinking down on the rock, and tightening her grip on the baby. "Not you!!"

He began to look distraught. His eyebrows gathered over his nose and his mouth began to pucker. She wanted to tell him it wasn't his fault he had been changed and that this adventure would help him back to his proper state as well. But he must leave her alone to get on with it. She pointed at her sister.

"You'll let Charlotte take the baby?" he asked eagerly. She nodded. He beckoned Charlotte over.

"You've to take Neri," he called.

Cautiously her sister advanced on her, so tense her feet barely touched the ground. Hesione stared out over the waves and, when she was close enough, held the baby out to her without a word. Charlotte took the child and hesitated.

"I'll come as soon as I can," Hesione told her sharply. "But you must all leave me quite alone for now. Go on. Go away!"

Charlotte backed off. Once she was with the group Hesione looked over to make sure she didn't hand the baby to anyone else. Then she saw something that brought her to her feet.

Some ten yards to the left and in front of her mother stood a tall, stout man. He was dressed in a navy blue suit, white shirt and a vivid brocade waiscoat. His face was a broad oval; his heavy jaw was clean-shaven; the long straight nose and small plump mouth were her own; the heavy auburn hair hanging over his forehead was Charlotte's.

Hesione scrambled over to him, tugging the fish-gut rope out of her pocket.

"You can't fool me!" she shouted, and siezed her arm. "You're not my father. My father's dead! You are my enemy — the one I've been waiting for!"

He looked at her shiftily. It was true; his eyes were wrong. They were dark brown and clouded with a blue film whereas her father's had been dark blue. Her long wait was over.

Now he had been discovered, she was sure he would do something. She hung onto his arm and waited. Nothing happened.

Then she noticed a dark grey spot on the creature's cheek. Her father had never had a spot like that and she was just about to say so when something moved in the spot. It turned into a hole, a maggot slipped out and dropped onto his lapel. The face turned from rosy to grey-green and crumpled. The skin broke out into brown flaky patches which split and oozed green pus. Under her clutching hand she felt the arm wither and soften and her fingers sank into flesh turned to slime till they encircled the bone.

"Patience and hot water will clean my hand," she thought and ignored the smell that drifted over her.

All at once her fingers were no longer wrapped round the bone, but round the dusty leg of a man-sized crane-fly. The facets of its vast eyes glittered and its fern-like proboscis quivered and drooled stickily; there was sticky grit on her hands and the segmented brown body was covered in coarse sand-coloured fur.

"You'll have to do better than that," said Hesione.

Instantly she found herself holding a blunt-headed lizard. It was deep, sooty black all over apart from an ash-coloured streak under its throat, and its fiery red eyes. The air around it shimmered with heat.

Hesione watched her hand as the smoke began to trickle out from under it. She could see the skin which touched the salamander turn red, and blisters bubbled up as she watched. The pain of burning travelled from her palm to her wrist and thence up the full length of her arm. It sank into flesh and ran through bone to become a deep, tormenting ache.

"I won't let go," she sobbed, "even though you destroy me. I'm done for anyway — but I won't let go!"

The smell of burning was shocking, but she put aside all her sensations for the thought, "don't let go."

At last she became aware that her skin was cooling. She looked down to see that she was clinging to the fin of an aquatic mammal. This was not the pretty brown seal of the sea-lochs, however, but a blubbery, ugly sea-elephant. The face had the pathetic, quizzical look of any animal trying to focus both eyes ahead. The muzzle was a horror. It was a long, grey, wrinkled nose which it folded into its face. It closed its nostrils with a loud sound of sucking, then lunged its nose out at her again. For an instant she recoiled at the whiskery monster, smelling of stale fish and fæces, but she took control of herself. The face smacked shut once more.

"It's going to dive," thought Hesione, and dragged her fish-gut bridle over the monster's head.

"Dive now, you bastard," she hissed, "and you'll have to take me with you."

Together they plunged over the basalt wall, and into the ebbing tide.

1 5

But doth change, into something rich and strange

As she hit the sea she felt a blow on her head, but managed to keep hold of the harness. She was dragged by the beast, half-conscious, for a mile or more until suddenly he sounded in a long, curving dive which cleared him of the harness and left her floating. Beneath her the bottom was covered with seething kelp and above the surface shimmered like an endless green blanket of cloud. She hung in silence between the ground and sky of a new country. There was no sign of the sea-elephant.

Her heart gave a single beat and fell still. Far to her left a black shape lifted off the bottom and started moving toward the deep.

"Hell and damnation," she thought, "it's him — it's the enemy and I'm stuck here."

She kicked her feet and waggled her arms but hardly moved while the beast made rapidly for the smokey horizon.

"Oooh, don't go!" she thought after him. "I don't know

how to get on down here. Mrs MacCrimmond said you would help me!"

In answer a voice in her head said,

"You shouldn't believe what you hear from her, or from the selkies. They'll say anything to get their own way."

To her relief he stopped moving away from her.

"I know they can't be trusted," she babbled her thoughts at him. "And the men are worse than the women — so cruel! The first time I met them they gave me a terrible fright. I couldn't find out what they were up to. They had this other poor creature as well — he was in chains and they were driving him along a tunnel. They said he was their king, but they were treating him like a prisoner."

All at once the sea-elephant was rushing toward her. Frantically she cried,

"What is it? Don't hurt me. I mean no harm to you. I only want to be rid of them. I thought you didn't like them."

He stopped and thought at her,

"Don't be afraid of me. The creature I saw in your mind just then — I think it was my brother. They captured him weeks ago and I've been trying to find him all this time. What can you tell me? Was he alright? Where did you see him?"

"It was a couple of weeks ago, or maybe three. I've no idea where it was and I'm afraid it was going badly with him. I think he was in pain...and he left a trail of blood in the tunnel."

Agony from the beast swept over her like a tidal wave. Quickly she added,

"Of course I didn't see him — it was dark — it may not have been as bad as that."

The beast shook his great head, communed with himself for a moment, then approached her slowly.

"I warned him. I told him he was taking unneccessary risks, but he never listens to me. Ahhh!!"

The wave of emotion rolled her over in the water.

"I'm sorry to have been so crude — telling you like that. It was thoughtless of me."

"There's no need to apologise," he said. He was close enough now for her to see him squinting at her sadly. He said,

"I should apologise to you, but I couldn't hear you on the dry-side and I didn't realise you were only looking for help. I thought you were a selkie, yourself."

Horror and indignation stormed through Hesione's mind and he calmed her down with a tinge of amusement.

"How was I to know you weren't. After all, you have one of their harnesses."

She dropped it as if it were red hot and it sank glimmering to the bottom.

"That's better," he said, "now — I want to help you — anyone on the run from the middle people and their disgusting habits will get my help, but I have to go on with the search for my brother. You do understand?"

She sent him the equivalent of a nod.

"All I can to for now is give you a tow as far as the bell-tower and leave you there. You know the people there, and they can set you on your road. Come along."

As she approached the bulky carcase her heart sank. She liked him and trusted him, but the idea of touching him again was repulsive. Also she was miserably aware that he knew what she was thinking.

"Courage, dear heart," he thought at her, "You can do it. Take a firm hold and don't be afraid."

Such generosity demanded as good a response so she grasped his flipper and slipped onto his back. Now that they were in the water his skin felt firm and slightly rough with a softness underneath that made it easy for her to grip with her knees. Grasping one of the rubbery, hairy folds behind his head she settled down, and they were off. In no time at all he spoke again.

"There's the bell-tower, now — straight ahead."

She looked up and saw the gleaming shape they were approaching. The sea-elephant dropped away from beneath her.

"I'll be off now," he said, "but as soon as I can I'll come by and check on your progress," and so saying he swam off at a furious pace.

Hesione looked at the bell-tower. The bell was not sounding, but the irritable green face appeared at the window.

"Oh, it's you again," it said discouragingly.

"Yes. I'm sorry I left so suddenly last time, but I had to go home. I wasn't doing very well at school anyway."

"That's because you weren't paying attention," it informed her.

"I'm sorry," she replied, crestfallen, "I never could listen to lectures. Besides, they didn't seem to be saying very much about my personal problems. They were talking about coral."

"Idiot! Of course it was about you. Why do you think your face was on the screen?"

"I thought it was because I was near the camera."

"Huh! H.C. said you were dim. Well, you'd better come in, now. We've got the elevator working again."

The green face backed out of the window and Hesione took it that she was to follow it into the tower. The opening hardly seemed big enough to admit her, but she had learned that the other world had flexible dimensions. She was surprised, therefore, when she stuck her head in through the window and found her shoulders firmly jammed.

"Use the bloody door!" screamed the face. "Round the back, at the foot of the tower. Jesus, what a nerd!"

Blushing hard enough to make the water round her face boil Hesione went where she was told and found the door opened and the green fish waiting inside it. It was a Ballan wrasse with a body much smaller than the size of the head indicated. She led Hesione through forest of arches to where a huge bubble appeared to be trapped in a tube made of meshed coral.

"In there," snapped the wrasse, indicating the bubble.

Hesione could see no obvious way in so she looked enquiringly at her guide.

"All you have to do is push," she said, tapping her fin and breaking out in white spots with irritation.

Hesione pressed her hand against the bubble's surface and it yielded a little then let her hand pass through. With a slight frisson of claustrophobia she slid the rest of herself after it and turned in time to see the wrasse pull down a small brass lever. At once she began to rise at a terrific rate, and accelerated so fiercely that she blacked out.

She woke to find herself lying on a hard, narrow but very clean bed in a narrow, brightly lit room. Her heart and breathing rate were back to normal. Looking round she found that the only other pieces of furniture were a dressing-table with a flaking mirror and a chair with a rush seat. There was no carpet and the window, through which golden light was pouring, had no curtains. When she sat up and turned she could see a skinny door in the corner, half-open to reveal a toilet and a wash-basin.

It came to her that she had been lying in this room for some days, but her memory of the time was vague as if it had been passed in a delirium. She searched through her mind for the sequence of events. James had been there at some time, she was sure. She thought she could remember him standing in the doorway at the foot of the bed looking down at her, but when she had tried to speak to him the words wouldn't come. Now, when she peered through the door all she could see in the dimness was the head of a stair.

Once, she recalled, she had felt itching on her forehead and leapt out of bed to look at it in the mirror. She found a bunch of spiders had embedded themselves in her head but when she tried to pull them out it had hurt them so much she had been forced to stop.

Someone had been feeding her. Trays of tasteless food kept appearing in front of her and she had tried to eat — without pleasure. Also someone had put her into a high-necked nightie with long sleeves, but she had no memory of the event. Tentatively she swung her legs out of the bed and stood up. There seemed to be no ill-effects so she tried walking to the dressing table. In the mirror she saw that there was a long gash in her forehead with the marks of stitches round it. It was nearly healed.

Next she looked out of the window but that told her nothing. All she could see was enamel blue sky and a white sun above, and far below a stretch of featureless white sand. Something about it rang a bell in her memory, however, and after some work she remembered what it was.

"I'm on the moon!" she cried aloud, and startled herself. Then a wave of misery engulfed her for she knew that the moon was a lonely and sterile place.

For many days she lay in the bed while the mysterious hands brought her food when she was not looking and took away the empty dishes. She dropped the habit of speaking to herself as the sound of her voice was distressing in the silence of the house. Sometimes she slept, though it never became dark, nor did the light change its angle perceptibly as the long moon day wore on. Then, one day, the tray of food was accompanied by her own, neatly folded clothes, and she put them on with a heavy heart. She had no desire to leave her room and face whatever bleakness lay outside and spent the days sitting on the bed, staring at the wall. The only thought that came to her was the observation that she was not thinking.

Somehow, as the time passed, she came back to herself. The depression lifted, if not completely, at least enough for her to find a splinter of curiosity irritating her. The time came when, drawing a deep breath, she stood up and walked through the door, her footsteps, loud on the bare lino, echoing ahead of her.

On the landing she paused and listened. The rest of the house promised to be as empty as her own room. The stairs were bare wood; the walls had no pictures; the light had no shade, and all was as clean as the day, many years ago, that it was made. She took off her shoes rather than hear the sound of her feet.

Padding the length of the landing she found a staircase that went up to a higher floor and two other doors. She opened the doors, and found only a bedroom furnished in the same style as her own, and a room full of tall objects hung with dust-sheets. Somehow the mute, shrouded objects frightened her and she fled back to the almost safety of her room.

There she stayed for one meal and one sleep, then curiosity overcame her again. Still shoeless she went to the stairs and mounted them to the floor above. She found two more small bedrooms and a third packed so densely with furniture she could hardly get in. The furniture indicated it had been designed for use as a parlour. Four cheap Edwardian dining chairs stood against the walls along with two display cabinets jammed with painted china mementoes of lost holidays. Two stuffed arm-chairs and a chaise-longue crowded round the fire. In the corner beside the window stood a large, round table covered with photographs, a potted plant and ugly models of houses made of shells. Heavy green plush curtains matched the bobbled table-cloth, and the walls were a paler shade of the same green hung with stained etchings. The effect was dispiriting.

The leaves of the plant, nevertheless, were shiny, nor was there dust in the folds of the curtains. The fire was neatly laid, ready to light. Someone had been taking care of it, yet there was no sign of the parlour ever being used. There was no wear on the seats, no holes in the rug, and no soot at the back of the fire, yet everything was so old that it should have been well worn.

Pondering this mystery she left the room and went through the hushed house to her bedroom. There she found her tray had been left on the dressing table and she nibbled absently on pale toast and runny marmalade while she thought about what she had found. She was sure she was alone in the house, but somehow there were attendants who kept things clean without showing themselves. She decided she needed more information and for the next few days she crept around the other floors. The house proved to be tall and thin, with no more than three small rooms — some bedrooms, some parlours — on each of its seven floors. In addition there was a silent, dust-free attic at the top and in the basement a chilly kitchen with rows of gleaming pans. There was no trace of life.

"Well," Hesione said at last, "my food has to come from somewhere. Not that kitchen, obviously — those pans have never so much as seen a fire — but from somewhere. I must find out where."

She decided to give her problem a holiday. It was time to take a break until some fresh approach occured to her. She went to see if any of the funny little parlours had something to read. Emboldened by her boredom she started in the one nearest her and tried pulling the dust sheet from a large square object that might have been a bookcase. It turned out to be a desk full of papers. She had been isolated for so long that it did not occur to her this might be an invasion of privacy. With no compunction she pulled out a wad of letters and began to read.

They were disappointing. Instead of letters she found that they were sheaves of notes on loose-leaf paper tied together with string. Some of the sheets were large and unfolded to reveal sketches of laboratory equipment on squared paper and dry-point etchings of anatomical preparations that seemed to have been torn from books. As she unfolded the last of these a handful of photographs fell into her lap. She was about to stuff the whole lot back in the desk, but the photos looked slightly interesting and she gave them a glance.

The next moment her attention was rivetted to them. Most of the pictures were old, sepia coloured and cardboard backed with crumbling edges. The first three were portraits of people in period clothes and she turned them over without interest. Then she found something different. It was a picture of a dissected out womb — a blind, featureless face with its blood vessels picked out in indian ink. She shivered and turned over the next. This was another monochrome, but black and white, and the details of it made her drop it into her lap as if it were soaked in acid. She sat for a moment rubbing together the thumb and forefinger that had been outraged by the contact. Then she stood up and shook all the papers from her lap onto the floor without touching them.

Back in her room she ate her supper — watery scrambled egg — took off her clothes and folded them repeatedly till she was sure they were in the right folds. She washed thoroughly, put on the crisp white nightie and got into bed. She lay still and screwed up her eyes to blank the image of the photograph from her mind but there was no help for it. As she lay in the unending light the details of the picture assembled themselves in front of her mind. No matter what she did she had to see what she was trying so hard not to see... a young man, it had to be a man... on an operating table...anæsthetic mask covering most of his face... his upper half covered by a green sheet... lower half exposed.....for... surgery... a large opening in his abdomen from navel to pubis... skin and muscle cut and peeled back to reveal a huge cavity and the sides of the wound held back by metal sutures..... a nearly spherical object about the size of an orange had been inserted and stitched into place..... but worse... her nausea nearly managed to crush the vision... thepenisexposedbythefoldedsheetandlyinglimpovertheman'sthigh wasunbelievablylong... absurdly long... over a disgusting foot long... she could almost laugh at the stupid filthy thing..... until she thought about the mind that lay behind the photos.

She lay awake for hours until exhaustion caught up with her and she slept to dream foul, repetitious dreams. Many times she woke with sweat running off her as she thought she heard voices on the landing, but every time she pulled herself awake there was only the empty, silent, golden-lit room.

At last she woke thoroughly and realised that the light was at last beginning to dim. And she had been wakened by a sound.

The sound was not one she could recall ever having heard before. It was a faint, rythmical clashing and chiming as if someone was striking a glass bell with a bundle of glass rods. For some unaccountable reason she sat bolt upright in terror and watched the door, frozen until she could see what was causing it. She was sure it was coming toward her up the stairs but she had no idea what to expect. Flight would be pointless — where was there to go? She had no option but to wait and watch the door with her eyes widening more each minute.

Then, in the doorway, in the fading light, stood an enormous sea-horse. He was about a meter tall, so far as she could guess. His head was capped with a cluster of gold filaments that looked very like a crew-cut; his body was pink and gold and red and ribbed down its full length, each rib being gold on top of red which faded to pink where it met his body. The effect was of a furious sunburn and that explained the irritation on his face. On his nose he had perched a gold-rimmed pince-nez. He was looking at her over it and opened his prim little mouth to say,

"You will have to come with me, now."

Hesione obeyed. Why be frightened of a giant sea-horse? She went over to the chair where she had put her clothes. The sea-horse backed off in alarm.

"I'll wait in the hall till you're dressed," he squeaked, and disappeared.

Wishing she had the time to wash some of the sweat from the night before off, she dressed and followed him through the door. He was careful to keep six feet between them as he led the way downstairs. He moved by coiling his tail into a spring and uncoiling it sharply to propel himself forwards. The chiming she had heard had been his tail hitting the ground. They went all the way down to the kitchen where the waning of the moon day made it necessary to switch on the light. The sea-horse jounced over to a door which she had previously opened and found to be an empty pantry. He butted the door open then butted the back of the cupboard which swung aside. Behind it a flight of steps led downward.

At the foot of the steps a narrow corridor led off in two directions. It was dark and empty, but she felt there was more life here than in the house for a faint humming of machinery surrounded her. The sea-horse set off at such a pace that she had to run to keep up with him. He was at home down here and seemed relaxed, almost jaunty, as he hopped along. They passed a number of doors, most of which were closed, but behind some of them she could hear voices and when occasionally they passed an open one she saw small offices full of papers and books. At one door she was tempted to pause by the sight of a great golden toad stooped over a desk, but she kept up with her guide. One door closed as they approached; one opened and two golden newts walked out carrying clip-boards and went through the door opposite. All this company left Hesione feeling elated.

"Go in there and put on the mask and gown," said the sea-horse.

He turned to go down the corridor, but she called him back. This was the first company she had had for a long time and she was not going to lose him so easily. He came back looking disapproving.

"Excuse me for asking, but how do you cope with being on dry land?"

His tight little mouth grew tighter. He said at last,

"It hasn't been easy, I assure you. To cast of the skin of my wet-side ancestors has brought me pain and danger. I've had to undergo many difficult operations and have come close to death at times, but with great courage I have persevered. Now I am quite accustomed to the lungs in my enlarged chest cavity. You see."

He inhaled deeply and went bright red all over.

"That's really splendid," she said, anxious to keep him. "So you think the struggles have been worthwhile?"

"Oh, yes," he said warmly, "the improvements to my state of mind have made the months of surgery and medication well worthwhile. You see I was never at home in the wet-side. In my true, inner self, I was always a dry-sider.

"And now, here I am," he simpered, "and I owe it all to Doctor Caddis. He is a genius. Without him none of this would have been possible. Only he understood how important it was for me to change."

"How wonderful for you," she gushed, "and do you think he'll be able to help me?"

"Oh, dear me, no. I would be deceiving you if I said so. You see, women are all so wet. Nothing personal you understand — but I don't see any hope for you."

She felt a pang of disappointment but shook it off at once. After all, she told herself, until a short while ago she had been expecting nothing but solitary confinement.

"I really must cut along now." said the sea-horse, "I have to see to my little ones. And Dr. Caddis is waiting for you."

As he spoke Hesione noticed that a slit had opened in his stomach and a tiny, suspicious pair of eyes were watching her from inside it. These were joined by another pair, and another.

"How many have you got in there," she asked.

He turned and hurried off into the darkness without answering. Sighing, she went in through the door he had indicated. Beyond it she found a changing room with a second door at the far end. On one side there was a bench where lay a surgical gown, cap and gloves, and under it a pair of rubber boots. She put them all on and pushed open the far door.

In contrast to the corridor the room beyond was high-ceilinged and brightly lit. As she stepped through the door her arms were seized and her ankles pinned.

"What the hell?" she gasped.

Her arms and ankles were held in padded metal clamps. A small screen swung out of the wall on a bracket and poised itself at her eye level.

"Please stand still," it said, "You will be inspected for inappropriate life-forms. It will not cause you any pain," and blanked out.

From overhead a cone on a flexible metal cable descended and began to nose all round her body, paying particular attention to her armpits and crotch. The screen glared again,

"You have failed to pass inspection," it informed her. "You will return to the changing room and swab yourself with the items provided."

Miserable, Hesione found herself released and returned to the cubicle. Large, moist pads of cotton wool packed in polythene lay on the bench. She could not remember if they had been there before, but she was sick with the thought that her personal hygiene was inadequate. Unpacked, the pads smelt foul but she did as she was told and returned through the door.

This time she ignored the inspection and looked about her. She appeared to be in something between a laboratory and an intensive care unit. Much of the floor was taken up with benches covered with the usual clutter of glass equipment, but against the far wall there stood a hospital bed. At its head a respirator hissed and clicked; on the left side a vital signs monitor winked steadily, and almost everywhere else were stands from which hung multi-coloured bags of liquid. The forest of gear was so dense she could not see if there was a patient on the bed. At the farthest end, beside racks of bottles, stood a tall man in a lab coat. He had his back to her and seemed unaware of her presence.

The inspection finished with a kind of mechanical sniff, and the screen informed her that she was now free to look around the lab, but she must not touch anything.

She wandered uncertainly toward a bench. On it there lay a board with a handle at the bottom like those she had seen in museums or stately homes with information about the item under scrutiny. She picked it up and read the type. It said,

'Hello,
this is a bench. It is made of wood. You will be able to observe the *bench-marks* — black spots where previous users have carelessly dropped acid. You will see no-one is sitting on the bench today because it is Sunday and even Magistrates have to stand up sometimes. Hah-hah. Geddit?'

Irritated, she slapped the board back onto the bench. Not even this noise attracted the attention of the man in the lab-coat. She strode up to him, determined to get some sense and said loudly,

"Excuse me!!"

He ignored her. She stared at his hunched back wondering if he were deaf but reluctant to touch him to get his attention. His lumpy body under the coat was abnormally wide and seemed to start beneath his head without the benefit of a neck. His hands and feet were covered in rubber gloves and boots. The only uncovered part of him was his head and that was covered in rough black hair. She was clearing her throat to try again when she noticed that there was an information board hanging from a piece of string round his waist. Gingerly, she picked it up and read,

'This is the great visionary scientist, Dr. Caddis.
He will not show you his face because he is afraid
he will scare you with his terrifying appearance.
This laboratory is his and it has taken him many
years to design and equip it. It is still far from having all the equipment necessary for his researches.
Still required are: a heart-lung machine; a dialysing
machine; and electro-encephalogram; a CAT-scan-
ner...'

"He wants to scan cats?" exclaimed Hesione.

'a brain-scanner; a sterilisation unit, and much,
much more. Donations left in the box beside the
changing-room door will be gratefully received.'

Confused, she made her way over to the bed. There was indeed a patient lying in it, covered to the neck with a green sheet, and most of his face invisible under a respirator mask. Tied to the bed was the inevitable board.

'This is Francis,' it announced, 'he is the doctor's latest subject and we have high hopes for him. He
has taken the surgery with great fortitude.'

She looked closely at the young face under the mask. It could be the young brother of the man in the photograph upstairs. She was startled when the doctor approached and emptied a hypodermic syringe into one of the bottles at the head of the bed. He still took no notice of her. She tried to count the tubes that led from the various suspended bottles, bags and cylinders to the young man's veins, but lost count after twenty.

"The poor thing," she said, and began to lower the information board. On the back was this remonstrance,

'Do not feel pity for Francis. He is a volunteer and a willing and a joyful one. He is glad to serve the Human Race by donating his body to the cause of Medical Science. He is the product of careful selective breeding, and much hormone stimulation.

'Think of the great destiny that awaits him. By this sacrifice he will free women everywhere from the appalling burden of childbirth and restore it to the duty of the sex which by virtue of its greater physical and moral strength is more suited to this task.

'His reward is knowing that he will be the first man to taste the joys of motherhood.

'Women will now be able to take their rightful place — they can recline, on their pedestals, perpetually pampered and free of all onerous commitments!!!

'Why don't you lift the sheet that covers him and have a look at what the great doctor has accomplished? You know you are agog with curiosity.

'Go on, have a good look. Women have such dirty minds...'

Hesione dropped the board.

"No, I couldn't!"

A red neon sign lit up over the life-signs machine. It said,

'GO ON!! HAVE A GOOD LOOK!!'

"No, no. I don't want to see," she insisted, "I know what it'll be like."

She turned and saw Dr. Caddis staring at her for the first time. He wore very thick glasses but she was sure he was looking at her, and that there was a malicious smile on his crumpled face. At last she fled back to the changing room.

Once in the cubicle she grabbed her clothes and began to pull them on with shaking hands. The trembling got so bad she had to sit on the bench with her tights and briefs in her hand and wait for it to stop. As she sat with her head pressed back against the wall a slip of card was pushed under the door from the lab. Reluctantly she picked it up and read,

'Think! You too could be freed at last from the necessity of sexual intercourse, childbirth and menstruation. All these sources of pain, misery and embarrassment will be wiped out of your life!

'All you have to do is undertake a short, routine operation which will cause you very little discomfort.

'AND YOU WILL BE ADVANCING THE CAUSE OF SCIENCE.

'Only think — without donors like yourself we cannot proceed with our great, humanitarian work.

'SURELY YOU CANNOT DENY SOMETHING WHICH WILL DO SO MUCH TO BENEFIT BOTH YOURSELF AND MANKIND?'

She finished dressing and pushed open the door to the lab. Dr. Caddis was standing outside the door and he flinched when he saw her. Aside from his goggling eyes, magnified by the glasses, there was nothing sinister in his appearance. She smiled her best smile at him. He retreated a step, then stopped and smiled hesitantly,

"You'll have to give me time to think about this," she said, waving the card, "it's a very big step — not something I could rush into — you do understand?" She was shouting as if he were deaf or stupid.

He looked crestfallen, and her heart melted in pity.

"Don't worry. I'm sure I'll soon get used to the idea."

He smiled brightly at her, showing blue gums. She closed the door and left through the changing room.

Back in the house she found it as silent as ever. It was

now full night, and the stairs, hallways, and her room were all lit by dismal little lightbulbs. She found she could not switch off the light in her room, but as it was already darker than she had been used to she realised she would not find it inconvenient to sleep with it on. She lay down in her clothes and let her mind try to grapple with the ideas Dr. Caddis had put there. Somehow she could not get to grips with them, and they kept slipping out of her grasp like wet bars of soap.

A rustling outside her door caught her attention and she sat up to see a young man staring at her. Finding himself observed he did not run away, but stepped right into the room and calmly studied her from head to foot. She stared back. He was golden-haired and tanned and dressed all in white. They exchanged gazes like this for some time until Hesione said,

"How do you turn these lights off?"

He did not respond but turned and beckoned to someone who had been hiding down the stairway. To Hesione's intense irritation five or six handsome young men crowded into the room and started studying her. She took this for only a moment before she said,

"I'm not your property, you know, even if one of you might get a part of me."

They looked blank and started to whisper behind their hands to each other. She lay back as calmly as she could and said,

"And if you don't show some manners right now, I will not give it up at all."

Still they did not answer her, but the whispering grew more agitated. Finally they left and pattered off down the stairs. She closed her eyes and tried to think again, with no success. At last she turned onto her side and fell into a doze.

She was wakened sharply by fresh noises from outside. Sitting up, she attuned her hearing, and heard voices coming up from one of the floors below. They were coming up to her room, she was sure, although she could not make out any words spoken, and as she listened she found that this time the voices were disturbingly familiar. She got up and went to the window.

The bleak landscape outside was bathed in pale blue light. Overhead swung the green, white and blue earth filling half the sky. Silently she went back to the door and listened. They were no more than two floors below, now and though they moved slowly she knew she had very little time to make up her mind. As the husky, throaty voices of the selkie men drifted up to her she took a desperate decision. She ran back to the window and threw it open.

"There's nothing else for it," she muttered, and climbed onto the window-ledge. As the first dark head appeared in the stairwell she leapt into space.

The earth rushed toward her and she could see that she was heading for the ocean. Rapidly she filled her lungs with several deep breaths and closed her mouth and eyes. She hit the water and surfaced quickly to find herself beside a buoy that swayed crazily in a choppy sea. The sides were strips of metal welded together to form a cage. In the cage, calmly eating sweets from a bag on his lap, there sat a boy of about eight years old. Hesione let her breath out in a rush and he turned at the sound. She caught a glimpse of what looked like another profile on the other side of his head, and swam round the buoy to see if it were so. There it was, another identical face, gazing, chewing, at the horizon. She said aloud,

"Yes, the two faces are exactly the same — small, neat nose, lightly freckled, pale grey eyes, dark eyelashes..." she swam round to the other side, "...pale brown hair, plump, kissable mouth.."

"Get tae Hell," said the buoy,

"Sorry, I didn't mean to offend..."

"Huh! Wimmin. They aye want to cuddle ye and slobber over ye — it'd make ye sick."

"How do I get to the bell-tower?" she asked. There was no way to smooth over her mistake.

"Juist grab my anchor chain an' haul yersel' down. It's just below here."

"Thanks," she said.

He turned both faces away from her and went back to staring at the horizon, his jaw working gently.

"You'll lose all your teeth before you're twenty," she told him, and sounded rapidly.

At the bell-tower she found the green wrasse at the window. When she came into sight it opened its jaw wide and yelled,

"Nyseeeeee!!!"

A damsel fish squirted suddenly out of a side window, overshot, corrected and pulled up at Hesione's face.

"Give them to her, then," snapped the wrasse, "I don't know — young things nowadays. They haven't a clue."

Hesione saw that the damsel fish was carrying a pair of lacy pink and white gills draped over her fin. These she thrust at Hesione explaining mentally,

"You'll have to put these on this time. Mother says that if you go on using bradycardia the dry-siders will interfere."

"What do you mean 'interfere'?"

"I don't know, but mother knows best."

Hes took the gills and slung them round her neck like a string of pearls.

"Fine," said the fish, "now press them against your jugular vessels — either side of your neck."

She complied and agony filled her for a moment.

"Ouch," she said, and her voice buzzed in her throat and burst out in bubbles through her mouth.

"You can inhale through these, and speak almost normally," said the damsel fish, "She invented them for her own use."

Hes noticed that the fish had turned bright mauve.

"Who is 'She'?" she asked.

"She is the Mer Maid. That's who you are going to see now," said the damsel fish enviously, "come on."

She led the way to the dark mass of the city Hes had noticed once before. At closer quarters the buildings were even bigger than she had thought and the vast, black shapes nearly obscured the luminous blue of the sea overhead. The entrances to the houses were on the top floor and the open doors shed beams of light into the darkness. At ground level there was nothing but masses of brown, shifting weed. Crowds were gathering in the streets above and darting in and out of the light from the doorways. Most of the individuals were piscene, but Hesione was sure she saw legs on at least one fleeting figure. Furthermore she herself seemed to arouse no interest among the crowds so she assumed dry-siders must be a fairly common sight in the city.

Nysee the damsel fish paused to check that she was following, then turned sharply and dived toward the basement of a house. There was a substantial gathering of fish at that point and Hes had trouble keeping up with her guide. There was a hole beneath her, dimly lit by a neon sign that said, 'M.M. — Tonite and Evri Nite'. She realised that was where Nysee had gone and dived after her. Through the hole she entered a cave where a shimmering blue notice said, 'Boops Boops Club — Members Only'. She stopped and looked for Nysee but she had vanished.

"Drat the girl," said Hesione, "whatever will I do now? I'm not a member. I've never even been in a night club before. I don't know what the score is. I hope it isn't too rough."

There was a roiling in a dark corner and a wrasse, brilliantly coloured, swept up to her.

"Miss Hesione?" he enquired, unctuously, "Please come right in. We've been expecting you. You are the special guest of the Mer Maid this evening. Please allow me to welcome you to the Boops Boops Club. Your table is this way."

"Why thank you," said Hes, and before she could stop herself she thought,

"I hope the pod-room here is cleaner than the one in the school."

The M.C. ushered her down a short rocky passage into an enormous cavern. The dark, craggy walls were dotted all over with lights — all but the wall at the far end. This was the blue of the night sea and she got the impression it was a window out onto the sea-bed. Neither of her guides were in sight now, so she sat on a rock near the door and watched for developments.

Looking round she saw that the lights were centres for clusters of fish. Most of these were bogue or saupe — shoaling fish — but she saw the occasional frilly fin of a gurnard and the odd pipe fish. The noise — a compound of clicking, buzzing and gurgling — was steady and loud. Occasionally a huge bubble would arise from a group gathered round a lamp and fly glittering and shaking to the roof. If a fish happened to be near it they would slap at it with their tail and break it into many pieces. This all seemed to be a sign of hilarity. Sometimes she thought she was the object of a fishy stare, but she could never be sure.

"I wish this was my idea of entertainment," she thought. "I might as well make a move."

Part swimming, part walking, she made her way the far end of the cavern to see if the view over the sea-bed was of any interest. When she got there she found that an apron in front of the window had been swept clear of rocks and weed. She bent over and hit it with her knuckles. It rang softly at her knock.

"It's made of metal," she thought.

All at once it began to move under her feet. She sprang upward hastily and hung in the water as a crack appeared at the edge of the metal sheet and began rapidly to spread. In the darkness of the chasm which opened beneath her she saw a huge black oyster shell. As soon as the last of the metal had slipped out of sight under the floor the shell started to move upward, shuddering slightly. As it rose it opened and a ponderous grating sound filled the club. This attracted the attention of the crowd, and their excited glittering grew even more strident, till, with a mightly clang, the shell reached the top of its climb and locked open. Spotlights came on, and there, in the white satin and pearl interior, lay the Mer Maid, smiling up at Hesione.

She was wearing a top hat, white waistcoat and black bow tie. In her hand she held a silver topped cane. Her hair, not blonde but deep red, rippled enticingly down her back. Instead of legs she had a handsome, silver and black mackerel tail.

The Mer Maid launched herself straightaway into a dance routine. She began by swishing high into the water over the shell where she executed a series of slow, curving figures, coiling herself round the streams of silver bubbles from her hair and mouth. Then she hung poised, rippling her body like a frond of weed.

Hesione was distressed by her own bad manners, but she could not bring herself to enjoy this display of vulgarity. The crowd, on the other hand, were rivetted by the performance and stayed still as death while it went on.

"Perhaps if I could hear music, I might enjoy it more," she thought.

Mer Maid's dance was reaching a climax as she moved off in a shower of silver and swept all round the club. Here and there she stroked a fin in a most suggestive manner, and sank to rest among a large group who went through several colour changes in delight. Then she burst free and tore back to the stage accompanied by rapturous clicks. She gave the crowd her famous, crinkle-eyed smile, doffed her hat, hunched her shoulders forward to emphasise her cleavage, and blew an incredibly big bubble. The crowd went wild.

Hesione stared at the stage. Mer Maid grabbed her by the hand.

"Come on, honey," she said, and towed her into the oyster shell.

The shell clanged shut, jolted alarmingly and dropped. When it stopped Mer Maid hauled Hes off the cushions where the violent motion had deposited her and pulled her into yet another tunnel. Hes felt a moment's irritation at the way everyone down here dived into holes without any hesitation. She could never be sure what she might find.

Red light fell across the tunnel from an opening on the right.

"That's my bedroom," called M.M. over her shoulder. Hesione took a quick look inside. The walls of this chamber were rough, like the cavern above, but there was an impression of richness afforded by uncut rubies, gold nuggets and baroque pearls embedded in them. In the far corner of the cave jewelled stalagmites and stalagtites joined to make a four-poster bed, which was hung with red and gold brocade. On the bed lay a green and black bull ray which must have measured more than ten feet across. His sting was draped languidly over one side of the bed, and his snout over the other. Hesione stopped to take a look.

I gave Hes a wave of the fin, but she only rippled her fingers in reply and backed out of the doorway like a zombie on speed. She's never seen me in the skin before, so I guess it was no wonder she didn't recognise me.

At the end of the passage M.M. had opened a bright doorway and Hes hurried through it after her. She was now in a room like a Homes and Gardens country cottage. There were frilled chintz covers on the couch and armchairs, a large stone fireplace with polished brass fire-irons, a hooked rug and a rocking-chair in front of it. Patchwork cushions filled every cranny and the frilly curtains were pulled back to reveal mullioned windows which opened onto the luminous blue of the sea.

"This is my very own place," announced the Mer Maid, and sighed a big fat bubble of satisfaction. "I made everything in here with my own hands — the soft furnishings, I mean."

Hesione raised her eyebrows in amazement.

"It's true," Mer Maid went on. "It wasn't generally known — it didn't suit my image — but during my first marriage I kept Joe's house just as neat and tidy as a new pin.

"Now — how about a little drink?"

"Thanks," said Hesione.

Mer Maid pulled a small trolley from behind the sofa. From it she took a clear plastic bag, attached it to a spigot on the side of the trolley and filled it with amber liquid. With a cocktail stick she dipped into a barrel and brought out a cherry.

"Sorry," she said, handing the bag to Hesione, "you have to take the cherry seperate. There's no way to get it into the drink."

Hesione hesitated, looking at the bag.

"You drink out of the spout," M.M. explained.

Hesione saw there was a little plastic tube in the side of the bag and put it to her mouth.

"It's a Manhattan," said M.M., "my favourite. Isn't it just delicious?"

Swallowing the sweet liquid, Hesione nodded,

"Very nice," she said, "but quite a kick."

Her hostess beamed.

"I guess you never had one before."

"No. Is it a cocktail?"

Mer Maid doubled up with laughter and a stream of bubbles coiled round her.

"Why you *are* a country mouse," she said.

"I don't drink much, if that's what you mean," said Hesione, bridling, "but I know what's what."

"Well don't you worry your pretty little head about my Manhattans. They can't get to you. Nothing down here can. I've done them all — valium, nembies — nothing happened. Have another?"

Startled, Hesione found that her drink was finished. M.M. took her sac, filled it swiftly then tossed it to her. It curved slowly through the clear water and Hcs had no trouble catching it. She drank half of it in one swallow. M.M. stretched herself out over the couch and sank onto it comfortably.

"Yeah," she went on, "I was the greatest little house-wife — just like you."

"Oh, I'm not houseproud. I just like things neat."

"Come on, honey. You can be honest with me." Mer Maid raised an admonitory finger. "Now, try it again. I know it ain't easy, but you have to try. You enjoy being a wife and mother — and God knows that's not a smart thing to say nowadays — but you've had the courage of your convictions and you've hung on in there. You were sure no-one could keep your "wee house" better than you did. But lately things have gone badly..."

Reluctantly, Hesione went on,

"Well, it's true. I feel as if I've failed at everything over the last few months — keeping house, minding the kids, even being pregnant — I just couldn't get it right. And then everyone else started doing it for me — and doing it better."

She looked down and saw that her second drink was finished. In spite of what M.M. had said her head was beginning to swim a little.

"At least you have your kids. That's something I couldn't do," said M.M. woefully.

"Oh, forgive me," said Hes, blushing. "I forgot about that. But even when you do have them you have to face the fact that one day they'll grow up and move away, and then where does that leave you?"

"Well, I figured that if you were good to them and liked them and showed them what was right they might leave town but they won't leave you.

"Anyway, you've got a husband — he's a good man. He'll stand by you. Won't he?"

Hesione was silent. She was aware that M.M. was smiling kindly at her but there was a haze settling round her brain. Somehow her drink had refilled itself. She took a swig and said,

"Yes, well — there you are again, you see. I'm not very good at it. I mean — sex. I'm sure it's nice enough, for most people — but really I don't see what the fuss is about. Most of the time I can't be bothered. And I think James must know. One day...he'll go somewhere else, where they're more welcoming, if you see what I mean. Oh, dear, I'm sure he will."

She was blushing so hard she could see the glow in front of her face. The queen of sex laughed and the scales on her tail shivered.

"Why, Honey Child, sex is easy for a kid like you. You just went and forgot your biggest erogenous zone."

"Where's that?" asked Hesione the boiled lobster.

"Your mind, darlin' — you gotta use your imagination — think about him. Think about makin' love. Think about his body and your body will do the rest."

"Oh."

M.M. sighed at her obtuseness.

"Look," she tried again, "you wouldn't start to cook a meal without thinking about it beforehand, would you. You'd take recipe books and you'd sit down and plan it. You'd decided what would go nicely with what — and if you'd never had a dish before you'd try it out or at least try to imagine what it would taste like. And before you know where you're at you're feeling real hungry. Right?"

"Yes."

"So the planning's part of the fun. Right?"

Hesione nodded.

"So for crying out loud, if you're going to share something with the most important person in your world why not give it some thought first?"

"I never thought of it like that. It just seemed like thinking dirty thoughts when my mind started to go...that way. Honestly, I don't think I'm a very sensual woman."

"Shark-shit," said M.M., "you're fastidious, aren't you? You don't mind admitting that?"

"No, I don't mind that. I have to admit it..."

"Well, there you are then."

"Where?"

"Don't you see? Fussiness is just sensuality with prickles on."

Hesione goggled so M.M. went on,

"Sensual folks can imagine what contact with anything would be like — they can look at things with their minds and feel it before they touch it. So you're finicky because you see all the nasty things and you can imagine what it would be like if they crawled all over you. But you like nice things, don't you?"

"Yes. Nice things."

"Well, there you go. You like your husband, don't you?"

Suddenly Hes thought of James's white body straight out of the shower and smelling of soap. And she caught her breath. Mer Maid giggled.

"See what I mean?"

"I think I might manage something, after all," said Hes. "God, what a relief I didn't give in to them."

Mer Maid stiffened and rose from the couch. She approached Hes, glowering.

"Didn't give in to who?"

"Dr. Caddis. He and his colleagues — they wanted to take all my female parts — you know."

"Dr. Caddis — you were up there with them? All of them?"

"Maybe there were more. I didn't stay around to find out. I threw myself out of the window," she added proudly.

"Gee, you didn't listen to them, did you?"

"It turned out alright. But he's got a very persuasive argument. It seemed to make sense at the time."

"You don't mean to tell me you agreed with that crazy old fruit?!"

"Oh, no. Not really — at least I don't think so. They didn't give me time to think about it," she bumbled, aware that M.M. was getting hostile. "I hadn't made my mind up to tell them off, but they just started to come for me so I went — out of the window." she repeated.

"You have got a long way to go," said Mer Maid contemptuously.

"How do you know?" cried Hester, "You don't know anything about it. Having babies isn't cute and it isn't easy like you see in the adverts or the women's magazines. You get all pulled out of shape, and you feel tired all the time. And they keep demanding your attention. You can't escape from them. And the rest of the world, men and women, both, all think they own a piece of you just because you're fertile. You get shoved about by everyone and you have no privacy at all. It's horrible!"

She could see she was making no headway. Stiff with rage M.M. said,

"If you want your privacy ruined, you should try being a star sometime. Every time you're sick or tired they're all over you wanting to know what's wrong. You can't even go down to the beach for a quiet afternoon on your own without a bunch of people hanging around waiting for you to fart. You're dead lucky, kid."

"Oh, I know, that was bad for you. But babies, you see. They don't just lie around looking gorgeous. They eat and puke and shit and you have to be around to clean it up. It's all so tying, and even when they're older, you have to be on tap. It's no fun, I can tell you."

M.M.'s tail was beginning to thrash. Through clenched teeth she said,

"Alright, Mrs Wiseguy, maybe I don't know about that but there's a helluva lot of things I do know that you haven't even begun to think about. So before we both say things we might regret I think you'd better get your tail out of here — so sorry, I forgot you haven't got a tail — not one that's any use to you — and go and get some experience of life in the raw."

Hesione was aware that nothing she could say now would improve things. She was too fuddled to think and M.M. was too angry to listen. Putting down her empty sac she blundered out of the door and heard it slam shut behind her. She struggled blindly back along the passage, up the shaft and into the night-club. No-one took any notice when she emerged and she slipped into the crowded cavern to sit and lick her wounds and try to sober up.

When she went past the bedroom door I saw she was really getting softened up. It was time for me to make my move. I got up and got dressed.

After a while she looked up and saw a grouper gazing at her. Its features reminded her of someone. She studied the wide mouth, sad clown's eyes and the folds round its neck until something fell into focus.

"Oh, good heavens," she thought, " — it's Ronnie."

"Beg pardon," said the grouper in her mind, "were you talking to me?"

"I'm sorry, I thought for a minute you were someone I knew from the dry-side."

"Ah! Would you have been glad to see him?"

"Oh, yes!" she said warmly.

She was pleased to see any friendly face in that weird world. The grouper's great drooping mouth swept upward in a grin of pleasure.

"Why don't you just pretend I am him, then? You look as if you could use a few laughs."

"Couldn't I though. That's just what I need — some homely company."

"Well," said the grouper, ruefully, "if homely's what you want you've come to the right person."

"I didn't mean it like that," she said, blushing again, but laughing with relief, "I just meant, you know, someone from back home. I've had a lonely time of it recently and it's nice to see a familiar face."

The grouper heaved himself over to her.

"I do so agree with you," he said, "East, West, Home's best — that's what I always say, don't you?"

"Yes. Oh, it is so nice to talk to someone normal. But I'm surprised to find you like home best. With a name like "grouper" I'd have thought you would be a gregarious type."

"No, dear, not me. Don't let the name deceive you. We groupers are all solitary, home-loving and devoted parents. All this," he waved a fin at the crowd of merry-makers, " — it's just a front. We like to seem part of the gang."

"That's funny," said Hes, "what you've said about yourself could be said of my friend as well. He acts the clown for everyone, but in fact he's daft about his family. He takes such good care of them his wife has nothing to do. She drinks."

As the significance of what she had said sank in, she felt a glow of satisfaction. She was not given to insights but now that she had tried it she found it was a pleasant experience. The grouper gave her a blank smile.

"I think you must be very nice," he said, "and sympathetic."

"I'm not, really," she admitted, "but I'm beginning to realise that everyone has their own problems dealing with the world. I should pay more attention to that and stop being scared of them all the time. You are very kind."

This graceful exchange was interrupted by a furious buzzing and clicking all around them. She looked up and saw the bogue, saupe and others going through all possible changes of colour combination. Some had fallen, stunned, to the floor of the cavern and were lying panting — their gill slits opening and closing frantically. The cause of the commotion seemed to be coming from the stage area. All over the night-club fish were jostling for a view of it. A whitening damsel fish sank past Hes and lay at her feet gasping,

"It's him! It's Ray. Oh, God, he's wonderful!"

Hes bent over her to ask her what was wrong when a gap appeared in the crowd and she had a clear view of the object of all this adulation. It was Mer Maid's lover, the bull ray. His eyes met hers across the cavern and she felt her knees turn to water.

"He's so masculine," squealed another damsel fish. "Oh, God, Ray, I love you!!!"

Hesione had to agree with her. He was standing in the spotlight, rippling the edges of his huge pectoral fins and nodding casually at the crowd of adoring fish who pressed round him. To Hesione he gave one, long look that told her all she could ever know about masculinity and power. Her heart raced as she realised he had noticed her alone in all this crowd — and she was not even one of his set! Her throat tightened.

The grouper nudged her side impatiently.

"Oh, do let's forget him," he was saying, "he gets all the attention, and he's not a nice person, really."

"I can believe that," she breathed.

"Listen," he said, eagerly, "why don't you come back to my place?"

She gave him a suspicious look.

"No — nothing like that. I mean would you like to come and meet my kids and their nanny. Maybe have a cup of cocoa? I've had enough of this place for one night, and I like your company."

On reflection Hesione thought it would be a very good idea to leave the night-club at this point. Assuming that she was reading the bull ray's looks correctly she thought the best place for her was out of his neighbourhood. There was nowhere else to go. She turned to the grouper and said,

"Thank you — I'd be delighted to come with you."

A gigantic eye appeared on the horizon.

"That's my place, now," said the happy grouper.

She looked at the homestead as they swam toward it

and saw that the iris of the eye was moving from side to side as if it was scanning the horizon.

"What a charming little place," she said uncertainly.

"I'm so glad you like it," he replied with one of his grins.

As they approached the eye the pupil contracted and the lids began to open.

"It doesn't want us," she thought.

"It always does that," answered her host. "It's a special security measure. Distrust everything first, until you can be certain it's friendly."

He swam right up to the eye and patted the cornea affectionately. The pupil dilated.

"You see," he said, "it knows its master."

He swam in through the aperture. Hesione followed and the pupil clamped shut behind her. The grouper broadcast a summons to the household,

"It's me, children. I'm back — and I've brought a visitor!"

Three small, striped fish with beards dived at them from a cranny. They circled them chirruping and nudging their father who laughed and shook his head. After teasing them for a bit he produced some pebbles from his mouth and the children snatched them up and swam away. Their father said,

"Those kids'll be the ruin of me. I can't bring them presents every night. They always know when I've brought them, too."

A voice from a cranny beside them said,

"That's because you always bring them a present, you silly man. You're just making a rod for your own back, spoiling them like that."

Into the narrow shaft of light from the eye-door swam a large angler fish. She was crusted with debris and had a tiny male clinging to her side.

"Men!" she said in disgust, "No idea how to treat children. Come along now, little ones. Daddy needs his rest. He's had a heavy night. Come on back into the parlour and we'll be getting on with our game."

She led the way through the crack in the wall and the children followed her grudgingly.

"You go along with them and introduce yourself," said the grouper, "I'll go and put the cocoa on. I love cocoa. You dry-siders have got some wonderful inventions.

"Go on in now, don't be shy. We don't stand on ceremony here. I won't be a jiff."

Dutifully she followed the family and entered a cave with a domed roof. She hovered around for a while, but introducing herself seemed easier said than done. Nanny and the kids were grouped round a small yellow patch in the middle of one wall and appeared to be arguing about a handful of stone slabs that were stuck to it. They took no notice of Hesione whatever. She reclined herself against a heap of weed-strewn rock and watched, wondering why she could only understand some of the creatures down here.

"Now, now," said nanny, failing her angling ray, "no cheating. If you cheat the alphabet crabs will eat your eyes out."

Hesione shuddered. The children continued clicking and started to ram each other, not playfully.

"Be quiet, will you," nanny insisted, " — you're making my head ache with your nonsense. If you'll promise to be quiet I'll read you one of those funny stories you like."

The children sank to the floor and nanny produced a magazine from the stuff piled on her back. Her eyes slid to the top of her head as she focussed on it and she said,

"Here's where I finished off last night —

His eyes met hers across the crowded night-club and Heather's knees turned to water. "He's so masculine" she thought. He stood there, in the spotlight, his magnificent pectoral muscles rippling under his olive skin and he nodded calmly at the rapturous applause of his fans. To Heather he gave one long look full of meaning that told her all she could ever know about maleness and power. Her heart raced as she realised that he had singled her out alone of all this crowd — and she was not even one of his set! Her throat tightened."

Hesione's throat tightened. Nanny went on,

"She had to get out of there. She dared not stay another minute in that club and give him the impression that she was prepared to accept his advances.

"Back in her modest flat she felt safe again. But this was to be short-lived. As she waited for the milk to heat for the cocoa the doorbell rang."

The doorbell rang.

"Heather's head swam in terror — it could only be him!"

Hesione's head swam in terror. She could guess who it was. There was no sound from the inner chambers. The grouper could not have heard the bell. Nanny and the children had, however, and they were fixing her with one-sided, fishy stares. Slowly she stood up, and when no-one else made a move, went into the vestibule.

The bull ray was hovering outside the pupil. She stood still, aghast.

"Can't I come in?" he asked. His voice was deep and vibrant, "Tut, tut, that's no way to treat a visitor."

To Hesione's horror the pupil started to dilate.

"This isn't my place," she managed to say — his air of masculinity was almost overpowering. "I'm staying with friends right now."

"Well, I'm sure he won't mind if I drop in for a few minutes."

"What makes you so sure it's a he?"

"Oh, come on," he said knowingly, "a pretty girl like you..?"

"It's not like that. I'm only here to see his children — really there's no more to it!"

He swept past her into the cranny.

"..and swept past her into the lounge," nanny was reading.

"Listen," said Hesione in a panic, "You can't come barging in here like that. I told you — this isn't my home."

"Ahh. So if it was your home I would be welcome to come barging in like anything?"

"No, of course not. Look, Mer Maid's my friend, I don't want to do anything that would upset her, especially as we didn't part on the best of terms."

"I didn't know you'd quarrelled with Mer Maid," said the bull ray.

" 'I didn't know you'd quarrelled with Marylin," said Ray, "but that wouldn't make any dif- ference...'"

"Mer Maid and I have an understanding. I'm free to take the occasional "sweetner" as we call it — a man needs to get around — its part of his manliness." He chuckled softly.

"Heather was non-plussed," read nanny.

Hesione was non-plussed.

"Well," she began primly, "you can have any sort of arrangement you like with her, but that doesn't mean to say that I'm going to be one of your "sweetners" — as you so charmingly put it. Quite the contrary."

"Oh, come on. You're wasting time trying to tell me you don't want it when all the time we both know you're dying for it."

"Rubbish!" she exploded, "I'm not one of those weak sort of women you seem to take me for. I know my own mind — and I know what I want, and I don't want *you*."

He laughed knowingly and before she could move his

tail flicked round and ripped down the front of her blouse and skirt. Another flick — her brassiere snapped in two and her briefs fell apart. A third flick and she stood naked under his arrogant gaze. He raked her with his eyes.

"He raked her with his eyes and Heather felt herself go limp under that penetrating stare. "You may not know what you want, young woman," he said hungrily, "but I'm damned sure I do!" and stepping forward, he enveloped her in his arms."

Hesione felt herself wrapped in bull ray's huge wings. His rippling underside squirmed over her and the sensation kicked her in the small of the back.

"Ooooh!" she breathed.

"You like that, don't you?" he murmured against her face.

"Mmmm!" she moaned.

His long tail curled round her leg and tickled her crotch. She moaned again and couldn't restrain herself from writhing sensually under his grip.

Nanny's voice grated on relentlessly,

"Heather felt herself dissolving under the assault of his skilled hands. She had determined that she would never give herself like this — surrendering to the attentions of one who was little more than a ruthless destroyer of women — yet deepening waves of pleasure were travelling through her and she was helpless under their pressure. She felt him slide into her and gasped as her loins burst into flame."

Overwhelmed by a whole new series of sensations, Hesione fell to the floor. Nanny went on,

"Heather's knees gave way and she started to sink to the ground. His arms went round her again, and this time there was a hint of gentleness behind the cruel masculine front.."

Lying in a heap on the floor Hesione looked up at Ray. He didn't offer to help her up.

"Did you er...enjoy that?" she asked in a shaking voice.

"Don't be ridiculous," he said, "you're a human female. I could never really groove with you — you're far too soggy and warm. Give me a nice cartilaginous fish momma any time."

He smiled lecherously at nanny who waved back.

"What's more you've only got one row of teeth." He smiled at nanny again and showed at least six. "No, no. I only screwed you because I like the feeling of conquest. It turns me on for a real piece of tail."

"Oh, you're disgusting!" sobbed Hesione and, turning her face into her shoulder, she wept aloud.

"I'm not disgusting," said Ray, "I just know what I want. If you didn't want me I wouldn't bother."

In spite of her distraction she noticed that he sounded genuinely puzzled. Suddenly a childish voice squalled, and Hesione found herself understanding him.

"I'm tired of fairy stories, nanny," he said, "can't you find us something really juicy."

"Be quiet, child," snapped nanny, "this is comedy. Shut up and watch — you might learn something."

"You're not to speak to me like that," yelped the child, "I'll tell my dad. Remember who pays your wages."

Nanny ignored him and went on conning the magazine.

"Dad!" shouted the child, "Daddy, come and tell nanny what to do! She keeps reading us these boring fantasies — we want something different!"

In an instant the grouper was in the room, his huge mouth agape and his eyes bulging furiously. But instead of addressing nanny he swam straight over to where Hesione was plucking at the remains of her clothing.

"YOU FILTHY CREATURE!!" he bellowed so hard that she was thrown to the floor again.

"I pick you up in a night-club, feeling sorry for you, and out of the goodness of my heart I bring you home for a bit of nice family living. I even introduce you to my darling children — and what do you do? You go and pollute — not just my home — with your depraved habits, but you go and do it right in front — RIGHT IN FRONT — of my darling children.

"HOW COULD YOU?!!"

Hesione shrugged her shoulders in despair. There was so much to say — so many protestations to make — so many injustices to name — that she didn't know where to begin. She pointed to Ray.

"It was him," she began, feebly, " — he came pushing his way in here and...forced...me"

"He wouldn't have come without encouragement!" shrieked the grouper. "I know him. He's a bit of a lad with the women but they keep throwing themselves at him. He's told me all about it."

The bull ray was gazing loftily at a point on the wall above everyone's heads.

"But you...you...!" the grouper rounded on Hes! "There's no excuse for you! You know better. Why, you don't even belong here! We try to make you welcome and this is what comes of it."

She shook her head and put her hands over her ears. There was nothing she could say that would make them believe her story. The grouper had drawn his conclusions and would not be budged. He came over to her now, snatched her arm in his mouth and dragged her to the doorway. It opened.

"Get out," he spat, "and don't ever let me catch you round here again," and with a shake of his head he tumbled her out of the door.

She lay on the ground in front of the eye and wept silently. Becoming aware of its baleful gaze she tried again to assemble her clothes around her, but the clothes never seemed to have belonged to her. A shadow passed over her and she looked up. There were two elephant seals gazing down at her — her old friend and his brother.

"What have you been up to?" he asked.

"I haven't been up to anything," shrilled Hesione. "Why does everyone assume I'm doing something wrong? It's most unfair. I came down here for help but all that's happened is that I've got into worse trouble."

"Oh, dearie, dearie me," said the beast, "you'd better tell us all about it."

Between sobs she told him all about her adventures to date.

"So you see," she concluded, "I really am more sinned against than sinning. Everyone has turned against me."

The elephant seal looked at her thoughtfully, his trunk writhing and shifting in his face.

"You are very confused," he remarked at last, "don't you see that you've betrayed yourself."

"I should have known you'd be against me too."

"Don't be childish. Why should I be against you? I'm an air-breather, myself. And I must say you look daft with those artificial gills on your neck. I suspect, young woman, you don't really know where you belong."

At that moment the pupil of the eye dilated and out of it swam the bull ray. Nanny was at his side and with a mixture of lust and protectiveness he swept his fin around her. Her mate was knocked off and fell to the ground helplessly rolling over and over. Nanny wriggled up against her escort and they swayed off into the dimness without a backward glance.

I was sorry to see the last of her. She was a good kid, but our times together were over. It was up to her now to sink or swim as best she could. Maybe I'll give her a call someday.

"I gather that was the villain of the last calamity," said the beast. "I can see why you ran into trouble with him

— he's very dashing."

Hesione ground her teeth.

"Do you condone rape?" she asked.

"Certainly not. But this wasn't rape like you have on the dry-side. He didn't take you against your will, he just read your mind and assumed that your body would go along with it."

"I didn't want him..."

"There you go again, lying to yourself. Your desires and impulses have been denied by their begetter. Now they're like abandoned children — with no-one taking responsibility for them they run wild and get into all sorts of scrapes."

"But that's awful. I can't go running around, giving in to any notion that takes my fancy."

"I don't suggest you should. What you should do is recognise them for what they are, take a good look at them and decide which of them are acceptable and which should be tidied away. You're good at tidying away but you will keep your eyes closed when you do it. You lose a lot of good stuff that way."

He spoke so kindly that she began to cry again. The two beasts sank to her side, full of concern.

"There now," said her friend, "there's no need for that. Not down here. It doesn't matter about mistakes down here. It's up on the dry-side you've got to worry about them. If you go on making them up there you'll become part of the middle kingdom and there will be no escape."

"You're right, of course," said Hesione, and clambered wearily to her feet. "I have had some hard lessons down here, but they won't count for anything if I don't make use of them back home. I suppose I'd better be getting back. I've got a lot to do.

"One thing before I go, though. Could I see the child — me — trapped in the reef. I'd like to see how she's getting on."

"Of course," he said, "me and the brother, here, we have to go up for a breather. We'll drop you off at the hermit's cave on the way."

Swiftly they carried her to the cavern and called in through the entrance,

"Visitor for you, H.C.. Don't be too hard on her — she's had a rough time."

The hermit appeared, an anemone bobbing rakishly on his shell like a nightcap.

"What's going on?" he grumbled, "can't a crab get a good night's sleep without pesky pinnidae crashing about?"

"Sorry to disturb you," said the sea-elephant, "but this is something of an emergency. This poor woman has had a series of acute encounters and she wants to see the effects on herself."

"Not another one," spluttered the crab, "I don't know what they're up to nowadays. Time was when people used to get enreefed and stick with it, but now hardly a day passes but some idiot turns up prying and making work for everyone."

"Oh, be quiet," said the beast and swung his snout at him. "It'll do you good. If people don't come and shake you up you get all stale and dopey. Look at you! When was the last time you changed your shell? You're a mess."

Furiously the crab raised himself on his claw-tips and started,

"You can't talk to me like that — I'm an amphibian not one of your damned..."

But the sea-elephants turned toward the surface and streamed off saying,

"We've got to blow — catch you later."

Hesione thought the crab was going to split his shell, but as the pinnidae vanished he turned to her with a sigh,

"You'd better come along, then," he muttered and hurried off.

In no time, it seemed, the vast side of the cell-block was towering over them and the crab pointed upward with his claw.

"Why were you monosyllabic with me, before," she asked.

"Trisyllabic."

"Okay, trisyllabic. Why wouldn't you talk to me?"

"Questionpest," he said, and scuttled off up the side of the building. She swam up behind him.

"What is this place, anyway?"

"Re-think tank,"

She chewed on that and nearly missed her floor. When she saw it she grabbed a rail, swung her feet up and somersaulted neatly onto the balcony outside her cell.

"That's more like it," she thought. "Now what have we here?"

She looked into the room where her childhood self still reclined in the tube of coral. It seemed to her that at least the edges of the tube no longer fitted quite so snugly round the tender body. The room was different also. The furnishings were no longer entirely white; a mahogany chaise longue had been added and a brilliant green shawl was draped over the back.

The crab scrambled over the edge of the balcony to join her and they went into the cell. It was true — the coral was looser. The child's hair was freed and floating behind her. In rapt silence Hesione stood beside the crab and watched. For the first time she was aware of the pressure of water on her skin. The crab was scratching under his shell.

"I'm glad I did that somersault," she told him, not caring about his reply, "I haven't done anything like that since I was younger than her." She nodded at the child. "At that age I was always climbing trees, swinging on rails and things like that."

"Why stop?" asked the crab indifferently.

"I suppose I decided it was time to stop being a monkey."

"More fool you."

"If I speak to her d'you think she can hear me?"

The crab shrugged his shell,

"Try it."

Hesione reached out toward the child with her mind.

"Can you hear me? I have a message for you, if you can hear it."

For answer the child's mouth twitched in a slight smile and a dainty string of bubbles rose from her hair as she nodded imperceptibly. Hesione waited. Slowly the grey eyes opened and the small mouth began to move.

"Listen," said Hesione, then stopped. She had so much to tell her she had no idea where to begin. Should she tell her about all the good things ahead of her that made all the other things worth putting up with — or about the things that could creep up on her while she wasn't looking? It seemed hopeless.

"I can't think of anything," she told the crab.

"She's too young to understand you," he offered.

"You're right. What's done can't be undone, no matter how much you want it to be."

The child smiled widely and raised her arms. Pieces of coral broke off and fell gently to the floor, revealing more of the smooth shoulders and the curve of a small breast.

"You are beautiful," said Hesione and, leaning forward, she kissed herself on the lips. "You'll be just fine."
More coral fell to her feet.

"That's all," rasped the crab.

She looked at him, bemused. He explained,

"You've done all you're competent for. We'll take over from here."

She noticed that his claws were covered with anemones like meaty bunches of flowers.

"That's right," he said, "we've been at this game a long

time. The anemones will dispose of the coral without hurting the child. You might do more harm. Now you run along and put your feet up in the waiting room. That's down in the basement. Carry on as far as you can down the steps, you can't miss it."

"Goodbye, then."

"Cheerio."

He waved an anemone at her merrily and turned to his task. Following his instructions she walked down the concrete steps to the cellar of the block and hauled open the heavy metal door marked, 'Waiting Room'. The room she found beyond was large and comfortless with cracked lino on the floor and dozens of metal chairs lining the walls and standing in the middle of the room. They were arranged so as to give a good view of the only expensive piece of furniture there — a television with an extra wide screen. The air was stale and dead. The windows, curtainless, looked out onto blackness.

Against the wall behind her was a small metal trolley with a few bottles of coloured liquid on the top shelf and some scratched plastic tumblers on the bottom one. She strolled over to it and read the labels on the bottles. They said, 'Manhattan', 'Pink Lady', 'Screwdriver', 'Orange Blossom', 'Maiden's Prayer', 'Gibson' and 'Bloody Mary'. She arranged them in a spectrum from bright red through pink to the palest — the clear Gibson — then took a tumbler and poured herself a belt from the bright Bloody Mary.

"These tumblers are horrible," she thought, "and where are the onions and the cherries?"

The vodka hit her abruptly and she had to sit down till the room stopped tilting. Vaguely she noticed that the television had come on. The sound echoed tinny in the empty room and she hurried over to turn down the volume.

"Where do I go from here?" she thought, "I suppose I'd best head home and see James. He will be worrying about me. God knows how long I've been away."

At the thought of her family maudlin tears started in her eyes. She went to the trolley and poured herself a shot from the Pink Lady bottle.

"Poor James," she said thickly, "there's lots worse than him. And he could have done better than me. Maybe he didn't think so — I did such a good job of conning him. Oh, dear..." she tottered back to the chair.

"It's not his fault I can't get up the nerve to do anything beyond my own four walls. It's me that lacks confidence — not him."

Suddenly a terrible silence fell inside her head. Somewhere in her mind a crystal had been thrown into some saturate solution and a whole mess of ideas and impressions stopped swirling around. The conclusion hung before her in a clear medium.

"I'm not really confident about what I do in the home either. If I truly believed I was getting it right there I might feel happier going out of it."

She slid off her chair and went to the trolley again. When she got back to her seat her mind had relapsed from its crystalline condition.

"Aah, so what? What could I ever find to do outside the house?"

For answer the television offered her hang-gliding. A faint mid-Atlantic-Scottish voice explained that for twelve pounds a hurl she could throw herself off the Campsie Hills. That had no appeal.

"I'm not the athletic type. There I go — ducking out — I'm no more or less athletic than any of the people doing that. It's merely that I don't believe I could do something requiring physical courage. It's nothing to do with my gender — lots of women do it.

"I could sail round the world like watsername. No — sailing takes a lot of money."

The television showed her a spiral mound of pink foam in an ice-cream glass. A bright red cherry dropped precisely into the middle of it and the mound swayed and bobbed prettily.

"Tits!" she exclaimed. "Can't they sell us something without using tits?!"

The telly showed her a woman twirling in her neighbour's kitchen, while stars glinted off the steel fittings. Then a woman in a skin-tight leotard hosed off teeth with a stream of white light — then a young man, with an air hovering between pomposity and menace, told her that his firm were light-years ahead of the rest of the world in electronics. The future, he implied, was going to be a strange, clean, lonely experience but he and users of his product would be able to cope because they were all young, clean and formidably intelligent.

"Cleanliness is next to Godliness," said Hesione and fumbled for the cocktail trolley. She was beginning to regret the effects of the drink for a kind of elastic ribbon was passing through her chest and down her arms. The outer two inches of her head had been turned into a rigid fuzz.

The television flashed her a single, flawless, woman's leg. The leg, sheathed in gleaming black nylon, emerged from a ceiling of black lace scallops, and had at its base a foot contorted so as to perch the heel on top of a thin black stilt. The shoe was kept on by straps of liquorice.

"Just the thing for chasing after small children. Bloody male fetishism. It's like Chinese foot-binding to stop women running away from the house. They put us in crippling footwear and tell us it's elegant and keep us where they want us. They tell us it makes us walk seductively and we fall for it. As if we needed any help. How they must hate us."

Snorting indignantly she bounced out of her chair to the window. As if in illustration of her point, a woman in high-heeled sandals hurried by. Her legs were a lot fleshier than the model on T.V. and her bottom jutted out awkwardly.

"There, you see," cried Hes in triumph, "they fire images at us about how we ought to look so we'll buy the package and we wind up looking Goadawful."

The woman, heedless of the wrath she was exciting, clicked off down the path to the main road. One arm hung straight in front of her and her thorax tilted forward.

"She's going to have persistent backache by the time she's sixty. And she'll have it because she was trying to live up to some alien standard of what makes her attractive."

Her tide of rage met a breakwater at this point. She was still sober enough to acknowledge that her husband was not one of 'them', and that he was by no means unique. But rhetoric is a heady brew and she mustered her thoughts to carry on, just or unjust.

"They marry us and expect us to pick up where Mammy left off. Aren't they ever supposed to grow up? If we didn't bath until we were told to, and swore and stayed out drinking, and didn't care if the shopping was done they'd call us crazy."

"What the hell are you gaun on about," said an irritable voice behind her. "An' what're you daein' drinkin' all the ginger?" it went on, even more irritably. "That's supposed to be fur our party."

Hesione emptied her glass and turned round slowly.

"Heh, nurse. Nurse! Gaunnae stop hir. She's drinkin' a' the ginger furra party!!"

Hesione gaped at the yelling woman. She was real and she was human. Ugly, certainly, with a shapeless white face and grey bristles on her chin — but most definitely human. And the others peeking round the door at them were also emphatically human. Then she noticed that she was breathing normally. Without noticing the journey she had been brought back to the dry-side.

"Where the hell am I?" she gasped, as a woman in a blue dress jabbed a needle into her arm.

1 6
How beauteous mankind is!

When she was allowed visitors it was left to James to explain what had happened. The day she had gone into the sea he had come home to find her gone, rung her mother, then both had rung the doctor. He had to admit that lately she had been getting difficult − acting out of character − and so forth, and he had to do something. There was the children to think of. She smiled to herself, realising that this was mostly an apology and let him carry on.

When they found her on the beach he had tried to talk to her but she dismissed him and consented only to give the baby to her sister. She seemed to think he was a threat to the child, and this had hurt him but he realised now that Hes wasn't really herself. It had been clear she was hallucinating when she grabbed hold of something invisible, shouted something about her father and then stood still with her hand out in front of her. She went very pale, lashed out with a piece of leather stuff and then went and threw herself into the sea. When they pulled her out the ambulance men were all set to take her to the General Hospital, because she was half-drowned and had a big cut on her head, but a Social Worker who had been summoned by the doctor said she should be committed because of the baby.

The hospital were sorry she had been kept in for Christmas but the sedation had been very strong and no-one could believe that such bizarre symptoms could have gone away so quickly. No-one, that is, but the old guy who wasn't given much credence in the hospital. He'd said all along that post-partum psychosis could clear up in a few weeks, but no-one had listened to him until after she came to herself. James was rather bitter.

"Don't worry about it," said Hesione, and spent as much time as she could with the old guy. He had grey hair, a sad, quizzical look and constantly sucked on a big meerschaum pipe. She liked him a lot.

She was discharged soon after New Year and at Ronnie's compulsory Hogmanay/Welcome Home Hester party she was handed round like a hot coal. There was a new face there — blue chin, heavy gold ring and rivetting dark eyes — who gave her a lot of eye contact. She thought fleetingly of the general reaction if she and the Dark Ravisher were to tear off a piece on the rug and smiled happily. Then she got on with being a good guest.

Ronnie fled when she told him how kind he'd been to her while she was away.

"What a bully he is," she mused. "Well, it was time he learned he hasn't the only option on embarrassing people."

As time went by she began to think that embarrassment was at the hub of most people's behaviour. On her welcome-back visit to James's parents she felt as if she was meeting them for the first time.

His mother let them in, as usual, and led them into the living-room where she sat at the table behind the settee

— the seat furthest away from her husband. Hesione took her place at the end of the settee with Neri. James put Robin down beside them and sat on the other side of the fire from his father. Mr Grieve struck a match and held it to his pipe.

"How are we?" asked Mrs Grieve.

"Better, thank you — much better," answered James for both of them.

"That's a blessing," said his mother.

His father's hand flapped, extinguishing the match.

"I'll go and put the kettle on," said Mrs Grieve. James sat silent. His father waved at the television.

"Lotta bloody rubbish."

James sighed. He and Hes had agreed that they should be candid about her illness with everyone which would have been fine if everyone could have been candid with them. Hesione saw he was hitching about in his chair as if he had to tell his parents about a bad school report, but she knew there was no way she could help him out. The silence stretched on until he finally blurted,

"It's not Hesione's fault she was ill. It was her glands — nothing to do with her. It made her see things strangely for a bit."

"I know that, son," said his father quietly. "It's one of those things women have sometimes."

James struggled on,

"It's like, see, when mother had the change of life. Er...you remember. She saw things all differently for a while."

"I wouldnae know anything about that, son," replied his father.

"But I remember it fine. You had to look after me. You and Sandra, you had to do everything about the house when she was bad."

"Aye, I did that. That's no tae say I kent what was happening tae her. She was aye greetin' — it was a bloody nuisance — that's what it was. I just had tae get on wi' it."

Hesione tried to catch James's eye, but he was stubborn.

"So you didn't care about her state of mind?"

"No' me. What good would that have been. She was haverin' about...That's a'."

An unsteady patch of sunlight appeared on the floor and swung across his slippers. He pulled his foot away. Mrs Grieve came out of the kitchen with a tray.

"Will you be staying till supper?" she asked, and added hastily, "You'll be most welcome."

"If that's alright," said Hesione, "we'd love to."

"Aye fine," said Mrs Grieve and ducked out. Hesione had the clear impression she was looking sheepish. Had she been listening at the door? As soon as she had gone Mr Grieve leaned over to James and, as if Hes wasn't in the room, he said,

"You don't want tae mess about wi' that sort of thing."

It was an instruction.

"I don't know about that," replied James looking at Hesione, "I think it's important to understand everything you can about your partner."

His father smiled sourly and knocked his pipe out in the ashtray. Mrs Grieve's head appeared round the kitchen door.

"I'm making sandwiches now for the supper so's not to bother with it later. Will gammon be alright for everyone?"

Hesione nodded brightly and the head vanished, only to reappear at once,

"Tea'll be ready in a minute," she said.

Hesione took the baby to the kitchen door to talk to granny but this did nothing to relax the good lady. Hesione sat down again.

Over the meal James tried a fresh assault.

217

"You should have come to the hospital. It was great, wasn't it, Hes? The gardens were really beautiful. The patients do a lot of the work, don't they Hes. You'd have liked it, dad."

His parents exchanged glances.

"Well you see, son," his mother began, "we've no car, and it's a kind of difficult place tae get tae."

"Ach," said James, "Billy Clarke would have brought you. God knows he owes you a few favours. It's not that far from here."

There was an ugly pause.

"Tae let you understand," his father said carefully, "we havenae told any of the neighbours where Hester's...been."

Hesione's vision clouded.

"I see," said James, " — well you needn't worry — your secret's safe with us."

His parents flinched.

Hesione was proud of her husband, but sorry to have ꞓ⁓en the cause of so much distress in the family. She spent the rest of the evening pushing the conversation along to prove that she was healthy, and when James came out of his silence to say it was time to take the kids home, she was glad to agree. Everyone seemed relieved, in fact, and Mr Grieve even got out of his chair to see them to the door. They left in an atmosphere of unforced jocularity.

"That was worse than I ever would have expected," said James as soon as they got into the car. "I really thought they would be more understanding than that. Can you forgive them."

"Don't say that. There's nothing to forgive. They can't help the way they feel — they're a different generation. They'll get over it in time. Don't try to rush it."

"I hope so," he said glumly.

"Just be glad you weren't home when mother and Char

brought the kids back."

"I know. I shouldn't have left you to it, but I had to get away."

"It was as well you did."

She was hoping to put his mind at rest. Her first interview with her family after her discharge had not been unpleasant, but it had been surprising.

Since they had taken on the care of the children for most of the time Helen and Charlotte had been more in touch with her progress than the Grieves. Furthermore, their professional training had given them a less super-stitious view of her condition. But on their first encounter she had noticed in both of them a certain shiftiness of manner. She had been saddened by this, and more than a little curious. Surely they could have approached her more openly? She decided to tackle this head-on while the encouraging words of her doctor friend were fresh in her mind.

"Now, ma, you know I'm not going to start biting the rug. Why are you treating me like this?"

"Of course I don't, dear. What a thing to say."

"Then why do you look as if you thought I might?"

"Nonsense – you've been ill – that's all."

"Say it often enough and you might come to believe it."

"Why shouldn't I believe it?"

"Hes, take it easy," her sister cut in. "The last two months have been rough on all of us, not just you. You're fine, now, and the prognosis is good, so why don't we all try and forget about it. Get back to normal."

"I'd love to do that," agreed Hesione, "but if you two keep looking at me sideways I'm not going to be able to."

"No-one's looking at you sideways. You're imagining things."

"My imagination is under my control, thank you – and my eyes are working well too. You both look ill-at-ease, and I need to know why."

"Look, leave it alone, will you," said Charlotte, controlling herself as well as ever. "You can't get at us for what happened. No-one was more upset than us. It's not our fault — what happened. It's no-one's fault."

"Blame you?" said Hesione, bewildered, " — who the hell's blaming you?"

"Well — I should have seen what was happening, for one," muttered Charlotte.

"Why should you have? You were busy — and anyway you work with normal people, not nut-cases. How could you have spotted it?"

"Yes, I didn't see you myself, but ma was worried...she rang me to talk about it and I told her there was nothing wrong. I suppose I couldn't be bothered. I know a bit about psychopathology — I should have used it."

"Charlotte, don't be so daft. Professionals are never expected to be objective about the people close to them. Who would have listened to you? I know I wouldn't. No-one could have seen this coming."

"Thanks," said Charlotte, wryly.

"I think I should have," said her mother and, startled, Hesione saw that her eyes were moist.

"Oh, damn," thought Hesione, "she really feels bad about this."

Her mother went on,

"If I'm honest — God knows I've had to be recently — I have to admit I always knew you were too withdrawn...after daddy died. You see..." she drew a shuddering breath, "I had no time to help you. I was too...disturbed myself, and I was desperate to make sure we had an income. You do see that, don't you? I should have taken time to see that you — both of you — were through the grief before I went off to work. But I had no choice."

Hesione wished her mother would stop looking so anguished. All at once she was no longer the shadow who stood between her and herself. She was a small, sad, sandy woman who had done the best job she could over the years, and who had never been sure that it was good enough. For the first time she walked over to her and put her arms round her protectively.

"Of course I see that. And we should have done more to help you — Char and me — instead of pulling away in our different directions. You see — you have to forgive us. But don't worry about me, now. I've learned a lot about myself. So in a sense the breakdown was useful. If it hadn't happened I might have gone on wrapped up in my...shell, and never broken out of it."

Her mother smiled up at her, tremulously.

"Is that true?" — she was genuinely asking for reassurance.

"Absolutely — isn't it, Char?"

Scowling furiously, Charlotte nodded.

"We'll have to do something about that occlusion," thought Hesione, "but later — much later."

She saw herself as a stone thrown into water — the centre of a mass of concentric circles rippling away from herself — meeting ripples from other people, and all making a complex and ever-growing pattern. For some reason she found this vision awe-inspiring, and she wanted time to meditate on it and assimilate it. She put it to the back of her mind for the moment.

Smiling at them both, she said,

"The old guy at the hospital said there was no point in pushing the blame onto anyone. Things happen the way they happen. We're all going to be fine as long as we're patient and honest with each other."

"Psychoanalysts!" said Charlotte in disgust.

Hesione smiled.

She put the children to bed. Robin had been slow to go to sleep, as he had been every night since her return. He seemed to worry in case she might vanish again in the middle of the night. She was not sorry, because her mother said that if he were indifferent he would be worse off in the long run. A little clinging would pass off once he found she wasn't going to desert him. She read him a story of giants and unicorns until he fell asleep.

"Char would say I'm corrupting his mind," she thought as she looked down at him. "What does she know? Most people have their fantasies and there are a lot far worse than these. Maybe if he gets into trouble one day an old unicorn will take him off and sort him out."

She ran a bath and immersed herself in it without fixing her hair up. It trailed in the water like weed and clung to her shoulders when she lay back. In her mind she addressed the sea-elephant.

"Time was when I would have been shocked to think of my hair getting coated with scum from my body."

"Indeed?" said the beast, politely.

Feeling a slight blockage in her nose Hesione inserted a forefinger and produced a long string of white mucous.

"Time was," she said, "when I would have been nauseated at the thought of that stuff touching my fingers."

"You're doing fine," said the beast.

"I think so too."

She wiped her finger on a tissue from the box beside

the bath and flicked it down the toilet.

"I can't be absolutely sure," she continued, "but I think I like myself — slime and all."

"Splendid," came the reply.

She rinsed her hair under the shower, climbed out and draped herself in her bathrobe. Back in the bedroom she opened the big jar of moisturiser and dug her hand deep into it. Cream gushed up beside her fingers. Slowly she clenched her fingers and squeezed the cream so that ribbons of it oozed out between her fingers. Then she did the same with her other hand.

When she had finished playing with the cream she stood and shook her bathrobe open. Starting at her navel, she rubbed gently in a circular motion till she was covered from thigh to shoulder with a fine coating of white, and paused only to smile at her nipples when they became obligingly hard.

"That should take care of it," she murmured, then shook herself back into her robe. She went downstairs in the dark.

James was still reading in front of the television. She stopped outside the door in a pool of moonlight. The walls were intact. Reaching forward, she pushed the door open with her fingertips and kept herself in the shaft of blue light. A faint smile came to her lips as she looked down at her pale, shiny body.

"James," she called softly, "come here a minute. I think I have something you'll find interesting."